Susanna Tamaro

Listen to my Voice

TRANSLATED
FROM THE ITALIAN
BY

John Cullen

Harvill *Secker*

Published by Harvill Secker 2008

2 4 6 8 10 9 7 5 3 1

Copyright © Susanna Tamaro 2006
English translation copyright © John Cullen 2008

First published with the title *Ascolta la mia voce* in 2006
by RCS Libri S.p.A., Milan

First published in Great Britain in 2008 by
HARVILL SECKER
Random House
20 Vauxhall Bridge Road
London SW1V 2SA

www.rbooks.co.uk

Addresses for companies within the Random House Group Limited can be found at:
www.randomhouse.co.uk/offices.htm

The Random House Group Limited Reg. No. 954009

A CIP catalogue record for this book is available from the British Library

ISBN 9781846550645

The Random House Group Limited supports The Forest Stewardship
Council (FSC), the leading international forest certification organisation.
All our titles that are printed on Greenpeace approved FSC certified
paper carry the FSC logo. Our paper procurement policy can be found at
www.rbooks.co.uk/environment

To Daisy Nathan
and to her questions a century long

Return unto me, and I will return unto you.

MALACHI 3:7

Prelude

1

Maybe it all started when you had the tree cut down.

You hadn't told me a thing about it – such matters didn't concern children – and so, one winter morning, while I was sitting in a classroom, listening with a profound sense of alienation as the teacher extolled the virtues of the lowest common multiple, a saw bit into the silvery-white bark; while I was dragging my feet in the corridor at break, chips of the tree's life rained down on the ants.

The devastation landed on me when I came home from school. In the yard, in the place where the walnut tree had stood, there was a black chasm; the lopped-off branches and the trunk, already sawed into three segments, lay dead on the ground; and a purple-faced man enveloped in the dirty smoke of diesel fuel was manoeuvring an excavator, whose huge jaws tore at the roots. The machine barked, snorted, reversed, and reared up, urged on by the curses of its operator. The damned roots didn't want to loosen their hold on the earth. They were deeper than anticipated, and much more stubborn.

For years and years, season after season, those roots had spread out silently, gaining ground little by little, entwining themselves with the roots of the oak and the cedar and the apple tree, even gathering into their inextricable embrace the gas and water mains. That's the reason why trees must be cut down: they work deviously in darkness, thwarting the labour of man, and man, faced with such pigheadedness, is forced to deploy technology.

All at once, under a cold winter sun, the tree's majestic umbrella of roots, with a constellation of little clods still clinging to them, rose up before my eyes – like a roof ripped off a house, or like the vault of the universe at the first blast of the Last Trump – leaving the deepest part of the taproot still buried in the ground.

Then – and only then – the man in the digger raised his fist skyward in a sign of victory, and you, already wearing your apron, applauded briefly.

Then – and only then – I, who hadn't opened my mouth or taken a step, felt my spine radiate into all things. My vertebrae and my marrow were no longer my own; they were part of an old, exposed wire, and its sparks flew in dissimulated delight from side to side, with cold, fierce energy. They spread out everywhere, like invisible spikes of ice with razor-sharp points, invading my bowels, piercing my heart, exploding in my brain, dancing suspended in its fluids; white slivers, dead man's bones, no dance but the dance of death; energy but not fire, not light, energy for some unforeseen, violent act; livid, scalding energy.

And after the lightning bolt, the darkness of deep night, the unquiet quiet of too much: of having seen too much, suffered too much, known too much. The quiet not of sleep, but of a brief death: when pain is too great, you have to die a little in order to be able to go on.

My tree – the tree I'd grown up with, the tree I'd been convinced would accompany me as the years passed, the tree under whose branches I'd believed I would raise my children – had been uprooted. Its fall had dragged many things down to ruin: my sleep, my happiness, my ostensibly carefree spirit. When the root finally cracked, the sound was an explosion; time was divided into before and after; light was different, shrouded in intermittent darkness. Daytime darkness, night-time darkness, midsummer darkness. And, out of the darkness, a certainty: grief was the swamp I was condemned to wander through.

The tiniest things are the greatest mystery of all. Protected by invisibility, the secret world explodes. A rock's a rock, before and after; it never stops being a rock. But a tree, before it's a tree, is a seed; man, before he's man, is a morula.

The greatest projects lie dozing in what's limited, in what's circumscribed.

When I understood this, all at once, I understood that small things have to be taken care of.

After the death of the big walnut tree, I wept for days. At first you tried to console me – how could chopping down a plant devastate a girl so utterly? You loved trees, too; you would never have done a thing like that to spite me. You'd decided it had to go because it was causing problems; it was too close to the house, and also to the cedar tree. Trees need space, you kept telling me, and besides, who knows, one day a root might have thrust its way up into the toilet bowl like a nautilus's tentacle, and surely I wouldn't have wanted such a frightening thing to happen! You were trying to make me laugh, or at least smile, but with scant success.

After the great eruption was over, I spent every day lying immobile on the floor of my room, staring at an obtuse, cement sky incapable of providing any clarification.

Shortly before, in one of my illustrated books, I'd read a story about sea cucumbers. They're harmless, faceless creatures that are nonetheless as stubbornly attached to life as any other living thing. When they're attacked, they expel the entire tangled mass of their internal organs all at once – heart, intestine, lungs, liver, reproductive organs – immobilising their predator in something like a gladiator's net and thus gaining enough time to reach safety, to take shelter in a forest of algae, where they can rest and allow their cells to aggregate and differentiate until they produce a perfect copy of the viscera they've discharged.

You see, I found myself in the same condition as a sea cucumber after an attack: emptied out. I had no words to say. I answered none of your many questions. We lived in two different worlds; good sense prevailed, on the whole, in yours, while mine was a universe of threats and darkness, occasionally pierced by lightning. The relationship between our two worlds was unambiguous: I could see yours, but you weren't capable of perceiving mine.

And therefore, on the third day, after your good sense had been exhausted, your patience overcome, and maybe even the paediatrician consulted, you opened the door of my room and said, 'Enough already! You're throwing a genuine tantrum. A tree's only a tree, and you can always plant another one.' Then you started busying yourself with housework, the way you probably did in the mornings when I was in school.

It's never been in my character to fling recriminations in someone's face. Nobody's to blame for interplanetary distances; they're due to various laws of gravitation. Everyone's horizon is different. You knew that, too: you always used to read *The Little Prince* to me, so you knew that every asteroid has its own kind of inhabitant. I felt a little dazed by your failure to think about the baobab, because the walnut tree was exactly like the baobab. The rosebush you insisted on buying for me afterwards couldn't take its place in any way.

A rosebush makes a striking appearance and gives off a pleasant scent, but then the rose gets clipped and stuck in a vase and finally winds up in the bin. But a beloved tree puts down roots around your heart. When the tree dies, the roots dry up and fall away, leaving behind minute but indelible scars to remember it by.

Anyone who imputes the bankruptcy of his own existence to another person – or to an event – is like a dog attached to a long chain that slides along a cable. Before long, the grass the dog walks on stops growing and the trodden earth turns dusty, strewn with bits of food and piles of excrement. When, worn out by endless pacing to nowhere, the dog eventually dies and his chain finally hangs down inert, all that remains of his anxious life is a sad rut in the ground.

Events and people aren't ballast, and they're not alleyways that you don't know the way out of; they're more like mirrors: small, large, convex, concave, wavy, distorting, cracked, or clouded, yet still capable of giving back a reflection and introducing us to a part of ourselves we don't yet know.

I must have awakened out of my sea cucumber's life on the fourth or fifth night. My room was invaded by the cold light of a full moon. The coat stand threw its sinister shadow on to the floor. Why must there be a shadow in darkness? What's the point of it, if not to evoke the existence of everything that can't be seized and held?

Often, during the evenings of my childhood, you'd sit beside my bed and tell me a story. Out of all that welter of princesses, enchantments, monstrous animals, and amazing feats, only two images have remained fixed in my memory: the wolves' yellow eyes, and the thudding, ungainly steps of the Golem. The wolves lay in ambush in the forest and along solitary roads, whereas the Golem could go anywhere; he knew how to open and close doors and climb stairs. He neither devoured children nor transformed them into monsters, but still he terrorised me more than any other creature. Whenever I recalled his name, the air I breathed turned to ice.

One early autumn night, damp but not cold, I felt

overwhelmed by those threatening shadows and decided to get up and go outside.

The air wafted a perfume that evoked a flash of summer. Maybe the scent came from the apples, some of them still hanging from their branches, others already rotting on the ground, or maybe from the yellow, barely ripe plums. Since the temperature hadn't yet gone below freezing, few leaves had fallen. The grass was still green, with a few wild cyclamens scattered here and there, as well as a couple of dandelions that had survived your resolute weeding.

By then, I figured all my entrails were gone. I went to the place where the walnut tree had stood and fell to my knees. The soil was damp and covered with little branches and twigs that had broken off when the tree came crashing down.

The air vibrated differently in the space where the tree used to be; for a moment, I had the impression that it was still there, its roots pumping sap up into the trunk and the dark fingers of the branches sending the sap back down. Not long before, nuts had dropped from that stream of energy anchored in the earth and outstretched toward the sky. The irregular symphony of their falling had accompanied every autumn of my young life; when I came home from school, I used to run to the tree and fill my pockets with them.

'Don't touch them, they're dirty,' you'd call from the

kitchen window, but I wouldn't obey you. I loved to open the walnuts delicately, taking care not to crush them. I wouldn't eat them; instead, I'd hold them in the palm of my hand and look at them. For some mysterious reason, they were absolutely identical to the ones I'd seen in our textbooks. Our brains — the brains of all mammals and all birds — are made the same way: the skull, like a shell, is there to protect the more fragile parts, the dura mater, the pia mater, and, between the two hemispheres, the oddity of the hippocampus.

Why did two things in nature resemble each other so strikingly? Why did one thing refer to another? Was this a universal law, or was it just an extravagance due to a moment of distraction?

The ground around me was covered with walnuts. Heavy rains had transformed the green husks of June into a blackish mush; all you had to do was rub it with your thumb, and the shell would appear. Hard, but not hard enough to escape the squirrels' pink paws and ivory teeth, or the beaks of the hooded crows, the ravens, the magpies, and the jays; hard, but not hard enough to avoid my questions.

Because that walnut tree — which was there one day and gone the next — had been my mirror, the first mirror of my life. Kneeling on the wounded earth, looking down into that chasm, immersed in the sinister moonlight with a seed in my hand and my heart seemingly empty, I suddenly understood that I would never, in all my time on earth, build mansions or amass a fortune or even have a family. As a cedar cone loudly struck the ground near me, I saw clearly that the path opening before me was the impassable and perpetually solitary path of the questioner.

2

When I recall our house, I see it suspended in the light of dawn. It's still autumn, because the ground starts to smoke and fog rises in the warmth of the sun's first rays. Like a bird in flight, I always look down at the house from above and far off; then I slowly draw nearer, observe the windows – how many are open, how many closed – and check the garden, the clothesline, the rust on the gate. I'm in no hurry to come down – it's as if I want to make sure that the house is really my house and the story my story.

It seems that migratory birds behave in the same way; they cover thousands of kilometres purposefully, yielding to no distraction, and then, when they reach the area where they were hatched the previous year, they start to check it out. Is the horse chestnut tree with the white flowers still there? And the green car? And the nice lady who always steps outside and shakes the crumbs off her tablecloth? They observe everything meticulously, because for months, in the African deserts, the images of that lady and that car have stayed in their minds. But there are plenty of nice ladies and green cars in the world, so what's the determining factor?

It's not a sight, but a smell, the combination of the smells that filled the air in the vicinity of their nests: if the scents of the lilac and the linden overlap for an instant, there it is, that's the house, we've come to the right place.

On the other hand, the odour that assailed me upon my return from the States was the smell of wet leaves that wouldn't burn; by then it was mid-morning, and our neighbour had made a big pile of them and was trying in vain to set it alight, filling the air with heavy white smoke.

And then you emerged from the smoke, perhaps just a bit thinner than I remembered.

Convinced that I'd be able to free myself from you if I put an ocean between us, I'd travelled for months, seen many things, and met many people, but all that distance had produced exactly the opposite effect.

I still hated you as much as ever. I felt like a fox with a great bushy tail: I'd inadvertently brushed against the fire, and it followed me everywhere; wherever I was, rage was in my heart, and pain, and the desire to escape the flames, which were always burning behind me, always bigger and more destructive. When I put the key into the gate, my tail was ablaze, crackling and sparking like a sheaf of dry hay, its brisk burning punctuated by sinister flares.

You were in the driveway, with a broom in your hands.

'It's you!' you exclaimed, dropping the broom. The wooden handle struck the paving stone with a hard, sharp sound.

'Obviously,' I replied, and without saying anything else, I went to my room, followed by Buck, who was yelping with joy.

In the course of the following weeks, our rituals of everyday ferocity went back into effect – I hated you, and you tried to avoid my hatred. On the days when you felt strong, you tried to blunt it, but your gestures were feeble, like an out-of-shape boxer's, and they succeeded only in irritating me further. 'What do you want?' I'd scream at you. 'Disappear!' I called you 'Old Woman'; I kicked doors while repeating, like a mantra, 'Drop dead drop dead drop dead drop dead drop dead . . .'

It's hard to understand how such hatred had taken shape in me. As with all complex emotions, it wasn't possible to attribute it to a single cause; it was due instead to a sequence of events that combined unfavourably with some innate predispositions.

When the first flashes of adolescence appeared what had been a tranquil stream in my early girlhood started changing into a rain-swollen river; the water was no longer green, it was yellow, and it roared around every obstacle. All sorts of refuse washed up in its inlets – hunks of polystyrene, small plastic bags, punctured soccer balls, naked doll torsos, torn branches, dead cats with bloated bellies – and everything bobbed about and collided weakly with everything else, impotent, resentful, unable to free itself. Since childhood, so many things had accumulated under the surface that neither of us was capable of seeing them: as the years passed, a word said or unsaid, one glare too many, an omitted embrace – the normal misunderstandings that form a part of any mutual relationship – had turned into two stores of gunpowder, one inside each of us.

'Us,' I said, but actually I should have said 'me', because you tried with all your might to avoid any explosion whatsoever.

You kept quiet if you thought that might work, you tried talking if you decided talking would be more effective, but both your silences and your words were always out of place. 'Why don't you say something?' I'd shout, irritated by some sign of inattention. 'Why don't you keep your mouth shut?' I'd roar, certain that what you were saying was intended only to provoke me.

Every so often, I'd have a crisis. Electricity invaded my brain; aggressive termites scurried around inside my skull. They turned off the lights, their little jaws chewed through the cables, and everything slipped into darkness. And then out of darkness and into calm at last, calm regained. Suddenly, there was no longer a river inside of me, but a lake, a little mountain lake. Fat trout moved sinuously in its depths, and the dawning light turned the surrounding peaks pink.

Yes, everything could really begin again, just as every day emerges from the night. The windows opened, and fresh air invaded the house; light entered with the air, and it seemed there were no more dark corners. We baked a pie together. We went shopping together or visited the library to choose some new books.

'Why not try taking your pills?' you said, and for two or three weeks, I obeyed you.

The weeks of tranquillity.

It was beautiful, during those weeks, to be able to breathe, walk, and look around without always hearing the fuse sizzling behind me; it was comforting to sleep and get up without the fear of exploding.

But like all beautiful things, it didn't last.

Suddenly, one morning, I opened my eyes, and the tedium of peace oppressed me. That linear, responsible life was no longer mine, and neither was the world of good sense, where actions followed one another as blithely as children playing ring-a-ring o' roses.

I needed pain in order to feel alive; it had to run through my veins like haemoglobin. It was the only way to a real existence. I knew it was acid, poisonous, a toxic cloud; I saw intuitively that it would corrupt my insides and everything I came into contact with; but I couldn't give it up. Kindness and rationality didn't have as much energy. They were limp, monotonous emotions without any real direction.

What was the use of being good? Of living a puppet's life, an existence like a sack of potatoes, inert victims of a more powerful will?

Besides, goodness, what was that, exactly? An indistinct sequence of innocent actions, the treacle that had to be waded through in order to attain some form of recompense, the odious chatter of afternoon talk shows. What could I do with such shoddy material? Nothing, nothing at all.

From dawn to sunset, I moved about as if I were an ambulatory volcanic cone. There was direct contact between my heart and the molten core, without the relief of meanders or vents or blind alleys; the incandescent magma heaved inside me, rising and falling in an irregular rhythm and sometimes spilling over, like water from a brimming container.

When I was ten or eleven or twelve years old, I could still sit beside you on the sofa and read a book, but by the time I was thirteen, my impatience started to show, and at fourteen the only story I really wanted to know anything about was my own.

On one of those very afternoons when we were reading together – it was April, and a cold rain was battering the garden – another person suddenly erupted from inside me. Our text was one of your favourites, *The Arabian Nights*. All at once, I stood up and snorted, 'I can't take this bullshit any more!'

Incredulous, you put the book down and said, 'Is that any way to talk?'

'I'll talk however I want,' I replied. Then I turned and left the room, slamming the door behind me.

Throughout my childhood, while other kids my age were soaking up TV programmes, you filled my life with tales and poems and fantastic stories. You loved books, and you wanted to transfer your passion to me – or maybe you were convinced that being nourished on beautiful things would constitute an antidote to horror.

From my first memory of our life in common there had always been a book between us. That was your way of conducting relationships; it was your world, the one you grew up in, the world of the Jewish bourgeoisie, who had abandoned the study of the Torah for the reading of novels. Books help us understand life better, you always said; through literature, we can comprehend emotions in depth.

Was that what I was rebelling against? Against your pretension of understanding things? Despite the great number of immortal personages who trod the territory of my dreams with daily regularity, I was becoming more and more restless, not more and more sensible. Was I rebelling against that? Why, instead of feeling emotions in depth, did I perceive their falsity?

It was as if, as the years passed, the scaffolding of our relationship had been built up by unskilled hands. In the beginning, the framework seemed solid, but then, as it grew taller, its defects began to show; a little wind was enough to make it sway. A great many characters had climbed up the scaffolding with me: Oliver Twist and Michael Strogoff, Aladdin and the Little Prince, the Little Mermaid and the Ugly Duckling, the Golem, and Hansel and Gretel's witch, White Fang's dog packs, Martin Eden, Urashima, and the benignly enormous deity Ganesh, who danced a wild dance with dybbuks and made the floor creak ominously. They were all there between you and me, some of them seated, others on their feet; their faces were superimposed on ours, and their bodies cast shadows on our story where I wanted light, the light of sincerity, the light of clarity.

The light that would allow me to gaze upon the only faces I really wanted to see: my parents'.

Yes, the period of my great agitation coincided with the reappearance of my mother. Up until then, her presence had remained discreetly in the background. There were only the two of us, you and me, and we were – or thought we were – self-sufficient in our relationship: no disagreements, no indiscreet questions, and the days slipping by like a fogbound train. Everything was muffled, deprived of any real depth; the constraint of the rails assured our peace.

Then, one May morning, I woke up and realised for the first time that there wasn't a single photograph of her in the whole house: not in the living room, not in the kitchen, no trace of her in your room, and you hadn't even had the good taste to put a picture of her in mine. To remind me of what she looked like, all I had was my memory, but I was little then, and as the years passed, her features started to fade like a drawing too long exposed to the light. They merged with other people's faces, other fragments of stories.

Who was my mother?

I knew only two things about her: she died after

crashing her car, and she attended the university in Padua but never got a degree.

That morning, I burst into the kitchen. You'd already heated the milk, and you were turning off the hob.

'We don't have any pictures of her!' I exclaimed.

'Pictures of whom?'

I heard a noise inside me that sounded like ice cracking underfoot. My throat trembled for an instant before I managed to say, 'Of Mamma.'

Two days later, a small picture frame appeared on my night table, and inside it there was a black-and-white photograph of a child dressed in a pretty little waffle-weave dress. She was sitting on a seesaw, the same seesaw with the red handles that was still standing outside in the yard. I picked up the picture and went to find you in the garden.

'I don't want your daughter,' I told you. 'I want my mother.'

Before I tore up the photograph, I had the time to read what was written on the back: *Ilaria, 11 yrs. old*.

After that, a Polaroid snapshot in uncertain colours appeared in my room. It showed a young woman in a smoke-filled nightclub. She was supporting her chin with one hand and seemed to be listening to someone.

3

Now I know that events can have different shades of meaning; what we see with our limited vision is almost always partial. Maybe you thought her memory would upset me, or maybe your grief was still too strong – barely ten years had passed – for you to be able to bear a photograph of her in the house. Maybe you preferred to keep her gaze and her face closed up in the depths of your heart. It was there that you'd raised an altar to her; it was there, in the darkness and silence, that you commemorated the awful tragedy of losing her.

In those days, however, with the Manichean rage of adolescence, I saw only a part of the reality: the cancellation. You'd lost a daughter, and you didn't want to remember her; what surer sign of a perverted heart could there be? And that daughter, moreover, was my mother, prematurely dead after a chiaroscuro life.

You'd told me practically nothing about her. Of course, I could have asked questions, and after a bit of awkwardness, you would surely have talked to me about her, and as you relived those moments, the ice around your heart would have melted, I would have given a name to my memories, and you would have been liberated from the burden of some of your own; and in the end we would have hugged each other and stayed like that a long time, our faces damp with tears, while the sun went down behind us and the things around us slipped into shadow.

I could have, but I didn't. It was a time of conflict, and so conflicts were what we had, in spades: wall against wall, steel against steel, marble, diamond. Whoever had the harder head and the fiercer heart would ultimately be the one to survive. In my obsession with imputing guilt, I was convinced that you'd acted like one of those animals who sometimes steal others' offspring and raise them as their own. You wanted to stay young, or maybe you envied your daughter, and therefore you'd taken away *her* daughter, her only joy. In short, I felt that your will had somehow meddled with my mother's life, with her life and with her death, because even for that – it seemed clear to me – you must have borne some secret responsibility.

Occasionally I think about how wonderful it would be if at a certain point in our childhood someone would take us aside, wave a long wand, and show us, as though on a wall map, the outline of the days to come in our lives. We'd sit there on stools, our heads tilted back, and listen to an older gentleman (I picture him with a white beard and a khaki suit; a geographer or a naturalist or something like that) explaining the surest route to the heart of that mysterious territory.

Why doesn't anyone ever give us any hints about when we should pay attention? The ice is thinner here and thicker there, go straight ahead, make a detour, back up, stop, avoid. Why must we always haul along behind us the weight of unmade gestures and unspoken sentences? That kiss I didn't give, that solitude I failed to assuage. Why do we live, from the moment of our birth, swaddled in this incredible obtuseness? Everything seems eternal to us, and our will reigns obstinately over that small, confused statelet called 'me', to whom we do homage as to a great sovereign. If we'd only open our eyes for a single second, we'd see that the ruler in question is actually a princeling out of an operetta, fickle, affected, incapable of dominating others or himself, and unable to see the world beyond his own boundaries, which, moreover, are but the mutable, narrow wings of a theatre stage.

How many months had passed since my return?

Three, maybe four. During those months, months of

guerrilla warfare, I didn't realise what was going on; I didn't notice that sometimes your step was uncertain or that your eyes would suddenly look lost for a few moments.

I got the first clue one morning when the bora was blowing hard. I'd gone out to buy bread and milk before the ground froze, and when I came back, you welcomed me with an astonished smile, clapping your hands: 'I've got some news for you; we have aliens in the kitchen!'

'What are you talking about?'

I didn't know whether to laugh or get angry.

'Don't you believe me? Come see for yourself. I'm not joking.'

We inspected the kitchen from top to bottom. You opened the drawers, the oven, and the refrigerator with steadily mounting anxiety. 'But they were here a second ago,' you kept saying. 'I tell you they were here. Now you're going to think I was trying to fool you.'

I stared at you in perplexity. 'Is this some sort of game?'

You seemed insulted. 'There were seven or eight of them,' you said. 'As soon as I lit the stove, they appeared among the hobs. When I turned off the gas, they moved into the sink.'

'And what were they doing?'

'Dancing. I didn't hear any music, but I'm sure they were dancing.'

'Maybe they escaped through the pipes.'

'The pipes? Yes, maybe. Maybe they come and go through the taps.'

From that day on, extraterrestrials began to live in the house along with the two of us. I explained, in vain, that aliens are launched from UFOs, that they can be seen only by NASA scientists or by people who have lifted too many glasses, and that it wasn't really possible for them to be dancing in someone's kitchen; had they made a landing in the yard, I said, all the neighbours would have noticed it, and the trees would have caught fire.

You listened to me calmly, but I could tell from the look in your eyes that you hadn't given up.

One day, I said, 'Rather than aliens, they seem to me to be dybbuks.' You shrugged your shoulders impatiently at this suggestion, as if to say, 'Call them whatever you like.'

According to your description, they were bright green – the colour of fresh peas – and they had the consistency of peapods as well; their arms and legs, however, were like the limbs of a gecko standing upright. Their tail was short and hairless, and instead of a nose and a mouth, they had a big trumpet, which they used for speaking, eating, and breathing. They appeared and disappeared at the most unexpected moments; they came down the chimney, swam in the bathtub, and waved their sticky little hands at us through the glass window of the washing machine. Sometimes you saw them flying about or scooting up the curtains like little marsupials, and soon they no longer limited themselves to dancing. 'They're laughing at me!' you said angrily, charging about with your hair undone.

You walked constantly, frenetically, all through the house, back and forth in the yard, without interruption, and even at night, which you'd never done before. You walked up and down the stairs, opened and closed drawers. Sometimes I felt as though I had a dancing mouse in the house, one of those mice with a genetic anomaly that causes it to run around incessantly, *click click click, click click click*.

Your steps marched through every one of my nights.

A couple of times, I got out of bed, grabbed you by the shoulders – they were thin and frail – and shook you, saying, 'What are you looking for?'

You stared at me proudly, almost haughtily. 'Can't you see? I'm trying to protect myself.'

At dawn one morning, already dressed and walking with a firm step, you headed for town. At eight o'clock, when the grocer came to open his shop, he found you waiting by the door.

Even before he raised the security shutter, you told him, 'I want something that'll work against UFOs.'

The grocer tried in vain to soothe you by suggesting

an anti-woodworm preparation, which could at least dislodge the creatures, or a liquid drain cleaner strong enough to drive any interlopers out of the plumbing. You slammed your little fist down on the counter, shouted 'Shame on you!' and left the shop in a rage.

After that day, when I went to do the shopping in town, people would often come up to me and ask with feigned indifference, 'So how's your grandma?'

4

In an abandoned house, decay proceeds slowly but inexorably; dust gathers; the walls start absorbing winter
cold and summer heat. The unventilated air grows stale,
and heat and humidity turn the house into a sauna. The
plaster crumbles into powder, and soon chunks of
mortar detach themselves from the walls and fall to the
floor with increasingly heavy thumps, like snow crashing
down from the roofs of houses when the thaw begins.
Meanwhile, gusts of wind – or, possibly, bored hood-
lums – reduce the windows to fragments. The effects
of meteorological changes now become more intense;
wind and rain enter freely, and so do the rays of the
hot summer sun, heaps of leaves, waste paper, pieces
of plastic, and small branches, accompanied by all kinds
of insects, birds, bats, and mice. Pigeon colonies nest on
the floor, while bumblebees build their nests on ceiling

beams and other creatures opt for the light fixtures. Accumulated excrement rots what's left of the floor, and gnawing rodents take care of the rest.

And so, what was once a pretty little house is now a building inhabited only by ghosts. No one would even think about opening *that* door. It's too dangerous; the continual influxes of water have rotted the joists, and a single step is enough to send you plummeting down to the floor below. Eventually, the floor collapses on its own, dragging with it everything that once made up the life of the house. The furniture falls, piece by piece, then, one by one, the glasses, the flower vases, the dishes, the photo albums, the overcoats, the shoes, the slippers, the books of poetry, the pictures of grandchildren, the travel souvenirs.

During those long, long months, the image of the house in decay was never far from my mind. I visualised a room, and then I saw it collapse, not all at once, but little by little. It was as if the surrounding reality had a different consistency, like quicksand or gelatin. Things fell, but instead of breaking apart, they were swallowed up by a silent void, in which the only movements were made by ghosts; they entered and left through the cracks, as agile as eels.

For years, perhaps for decades, aliens had been dozing in some nook of your brain, probably deposited there by a documentary on extraterrestrials. In any case, these creatures – with suckers on their little feet and a combination mouth and nose shaped like a trumpet – had entered your head and lodged there secretly, never giving a sign of life. While you were cooking or talking or driving a car or reading books or listening to music or reciting poetry, that little colony was suspended in a state between sleep and waking, waiting for the hinges to give way, for a gust of wind stronger than the others to set them free.

Yes, the aliens-dybbuks were the bugle call. I should have been alarmed by those first signs and prepared myself for battle; instead, I didn't even put on my armour. I couldn't imagine that our domestic skirmishes would change in any way, or that I'd go from being the ambusher to being ambushed myself, and by an invisible enemy who was active on both fronts.

I had to defend myself, and I had to defend you, too. Day after day, your memory sagged a little more, collapsing like the floor joists in the abandoned house.

As your memory collapsed, it was filled with ghosts.

After a certain point, there was a throng between you and me. We lived with that sinister company, and the floor beneath our feet was as sheer and translucent as a sheet of thin pastry.

A few months after the appearance of the UFOs, I called the doctor – for myself, I pretended, so as not to alarm you.

That day, you behaved in an absolutely normal way. You put a table under the pavilion in the garden, spread a lovely tablecloth over it, and after setting out plates and cutlery, you offered the doctor, your old friend, some biscotti and cold tea. He asked you a few questions, nonchalantly, and you answered them happily. Then the two of you started talking about the upcoming holidays, about one of the doctor's grandchildren, who was coming to stay with him, and about the best way to combat aphids on roses. You'd been told that the cheapest and most effective method was to steep cigarette butts in water and spray the aphids with that.

'Exactly!' the doctor cried. 'If they kill us, they'll kill aphids, too.'

I looked at you and felt bewildered. What had happened to the unwelcome guests in the kitchen?

At the end of the lawn, a blackbird was insistently laying claim to its territory, and a cloud of midges danced over a particularly moist flowerbed. The light of the setting sun struck their wings, transforming them into flakes of gold. When a stag-beetle made a noisy pass over our table, you stood up and said, 'I'll give you a few minutes of privacy – my hydrangeas need watering.'

We silently followed you with our eyes as you picked

up one end of the hose and walked over to the tap. Buck ran after you, barking at the black rubber tube sliding through the grass. Was he playing a game? Did he really think he was protecting you? Who knows?

Once we were alone, it didn't take much of an effort for me to convince the doctor that your calm, normal behaviour was more apparent than real. Sufferers from diseases that affect memory and personality retain a semblance of control at first, he explained. They make an unconscious effort to behave as they always have in front of outsiders; it's as though a kind of extraordinary modesty comes down to protect the sick person.

You'd already had a stroke while I was in the States, the doctor told me – didn't I know about that? – and there'd probably been some other ischaemic episodes; the blood supply to your brain was steadily decreasing, and the hippocampus was getting wobbly. Initially, days disappeared from your memory, then months, then years, voices, faces, swept away as though by a series of tsunamis: every wave carried off a detail and bore it out into the open sea, into the ocean, to a place from which it was impossible to return. The few things capable of resisting were nonetheless disfigured by the violence of the impact.

You were still watering the flowers. We could see the movements of your silhouette, surrounded by a cloud of gleaming water droplets suspended in light.

'Is it treatable?' I asked.

'Not very. There are tranquillisers that have some effect.'

'And how long will her condition last?'

'As long as her heart holds out. It sounds cruel, but that's the way it is. The head goes away; the heart stands its ground. It can beat for years inside a body that's become an empty shell.'

When I walked the doctor to the gate, you waved goodbye to him from a distance with an open hand, like a little girl going off on a school trip.

The day ended without surprises. After watering the garden, you went back inside and fixed dinner. The first summer breeze — fragrant, warm, laden with hope — came through the open windows. We talked about books; you wanted to reread *Buddenbrooks*. 'Isn't it boring?' I asked you. 'Not in the slightest!' you replied, and you started telling me about the brewer, Permaneder, his wife, and all the other characters, who had remained in your memory all those years.

Before going to bed, we exchanged goodnight kisses. We hadn't done that for a long time, not since before I'd left for America.

In bed I considered the possibility that you'd been joking; you'd had a good time, you'd pulled a fast one on me, and now the game was over. I fell asleep with that thought.

The following morning, I woke up suddenly. Your enraged face was very close to mine, and you said, 'You've stolen my slippers!'

Over the course of the next few weeks, I found myself cohabiting with a complete stranger. The extraterrestrials had disappeared, but their place had been taken by a persecution complex. Everything and everyone was conspiring against you.

It was a conspiracy made up of malevolent whispers, behind-the-back mockery, constant petty theft: your slippers and your dressing gown disappeared; your handbag and your overcoat vanished into thin air; your keys and your glasses slid into the void for ever. Someone stole the pot you wanted to cook in and the lunch you had just prepared. In the refrigerator, there was no trace of the things you'd bought at the store, and the soap was missing from the bathroom. Given that the UFOs and their occupants were no longer around, the person solely responsible for all this wanton pilfering was me, always and only me. I did it just to spite you, to turn your life into a torment of infernal little searches.

You bought a great many chains and padlocks from the hardware store and used them to bind and lock everything. In order to keep from losing the various keys, you strung them on a long red ribbon, which you wore around your neck. In my memory, the incessant jangling of your keys, coupled with the pitter-patter of your indefatigable footsteps, is the background sound of those months.

You accused me of the most incredible things, and I didn't know how to defend myself. The words I tried to say were like an inflammable liquid – just a few drops were enough to make you explode. You'd burst into flames of rage, your jaw clenched, your eyes narrow, your thin hands scratching the air; you'd spend hours spouting unrepeatable curses. You opened and closed all the drawers, furtively carrying off various objects to new and even more secret places. You opened and closed the armoires, the refrigerator, the oven. You went up and down the stairs. You opened and closed the windows, suddenly sticking your head out in order to catch someone in the act of lying in wait for you. You did the same thing with the front door. You were sure you'd seen someone; presences hidden behind the jambs, scrutinising you with malevolent eyes. They had to be fought ruthlessly, implacably. They had to be beaten to the punch.

In an attempt to show some solidarity with you, I helped you organise your various defensive strategies. I bought a whistle and told you it was endowed with magical powers; it could keep malignant entities at a distance. You snatched it out of my hand, wide-eyed with amazement. 'Really? It works?' you kept saying, repeating the words with a sort of relieved gratitude.

Indeed, it *did* work for a certain period of time. A new household sound joined your footfalls and the jangling of your improvised key ring: the piercing shriek of that whistle, instantly accompanied by Buck's howling – the high frequencies disturbed him. And there I was, roaming about like a ghost in the midst of this diabolical symphony. During the rare periods when you yielded to sleep, I stood beside your bed and studied you. You were coiled up in a defensive position, with clenched fists and tense lips; your facial muscles moved and twitched ceaselessly, and so did your eyes behind the thin veil of your eyelids.

Contemplating your features, I tried to see in them the person who had raised me. What had happened to her? Who was this old woman I was looking at? Where had she come from? How was it possible for a mild, gentle, matronly lady to turn into her opposite? Meanness, rage, suspicion, violence – what was all that? What had caused such an explosion of awfulness? Had it always lain smouldering inside her? Had she simply managed to control it for all those years, and now, having shed the inhibitions of mental health, was she revealing the person she'd always wanted to be? Or had she really been taken over by a dybbuk? Was there a possibility that this dybbuk would invade me, too?

Or do we, right from the start, like creatures in certain science-fiction movies, perhaps contain – hidden between the pia mater and the dura mater – a program coded for self-destruction? Who sets the timer? Who determines the length of the program?

I had never given much thought to whether or not the heavens were inhabited by Someone different from the UFOs and the extraterrestrials that flew in them, but during the course of those long autumn afternoons, pondering this question for the first time, I reached a conclusion: the heavens are empty, or if they're not, the entity that inhabits them is thoroughly uninterested in what's going on in the world below. This was a being, I thought, who must have been distracted frequently while creating his little toy. How else to explain the fact that a person could bear such deterioration? That a life full of dignity and intelligence could be brought so low in just a few months? That memory could disappear just like that, as though a sponge had been passed over it? What hypocrites they must be, the people who talked about our dear Heavenly Father! What father would ever want such a fate for his children?

Often, at night – trying to escape the constant clicking of your footsteps, the screech of your whistle, the squealing of unoiled hinges – I took refuge in the farthest corner of the yard.

Seen from outside, the house really did look like a

ghost ship. First I'd hear the jangling keys, and then I'd see you appear and disappear like a shadow behind the lighted windows; and all the while, the roar of the heavy goods traffic on the highway mounted to my ears, echoing the lonesome barking of the dogs in the scattered country houses.

On windy nights, the black pines above my head creaked and groaned like the masts on a ship.

I crouched at their feet, and at last, I was able to cry – in anger more than sorrow. From weeping, I passed to kicking; I struck their trunks violently with my feet, and then I punched the bark until blood ran down my wrist. 'Let me die!' I screamed into the wind, raising my voice so that my words would be carried high and far. 'Let her die! Carry her off, destroy her, pulverise her! If you don't want her, then at least take me! Yes, if You exist, You up there, let me die!' Then I threw myself on the ground and hugged Buck, who'd been standing terrified at my feet, wagging his tail.

One morning, on waking up from one of those alfresco nights, I was afraid my prayers had been heard. I'd slept later than usual, and when I went back into the house, an unusual stillness reigned. There was no sound of shuffling feet, no whistle, no jangling keys, no cursing. Nothing.

After a few minutes of incredulous waiting, I carefully cracked the door of your room, afraid that I would find your body there. The same fear tugged at me as I searched through every room in the house, but there was no trace of you.

Then, followed by Buck, I went out into the yard, but you weren't among the geraniums, nor in the woodshed, nor even in the garage. You couldn't have taken the car, because your keys had gone missing some time ago; therefore, if you'd left, you had to have done so on foot, although your coat was in its usual spot, and so was the handbag you were never without.

I was about to go to the police and report your disappearance when the telephone rang. It was the fruit vendor. He'd stopped you while you were crossing an intersection – barefoot and wearing only your slip – and taken you into his shop.

'We're in the tunnel,' you kept saying. 'Papa, Mamma, we're in the tunnel. We made it!'

For some time, you'd been obsessed with shelling, and with Germans beating on the door. When you saw me, you turned hostile, but you gave no sign of recognition. 'What do you want from me?' you asked. Only when I whispered in your ear that I was the person in charge of air defence did you give me your hand and follow me back to the house, as docile as a weary child.

From that morning on, all our domestic emergencies

involved your flights from the house and your heedless gestures. You washed your hands over the gas burner; if you felt like eating some marmalade, you didn't open the jar, you broke it, and then you necessarily swallowed bits of glass, too; if you locked yourself in a room for protection, you shouted that we had to run to the shelter, because the alarm had already sounded; when Buck appeared at the door, you yelled, 'The Gestapo are coming!' – perhaps because of his extremely distant resemblance to an Alsatian – and then you'd run and hide, your face wet with tears.

As far as you were concerned, I stopped being a hostile person and became a complete stranger; you never knew who I was. During those months, in order to survive and to help you to survive, I turned myself (like one of your favourite characters, Aladdin's genie) into a multitude of different people.

The game ended one windy December morning. Coming back from shopping, I found you on the ground in the yard, still wearing your nightgown. Your bare feet were covered with dirt, and Buck was whining by your side. Pursued by one of your ghosts, you'd run out of the house, probably tripped over some root, and struck your head against a tree. You were lying supine and smiling, one arm flung out over your head, as though doing the backstroke through the grass. A thin stream of blood marked your forehead, and beneath your eyelids, your eyes were finally at rest.

5

Not that morning, but three days later, you died in a ward of the hospital.

Before dawn, while I was tossing and turning on my bed at home, the angel of death, armed with his fiery sword, swooped down on you. Buck must have sensed his passage, because when I got up, he wasn't waiting for me, as usual, by the back door. Since he often disappeared, I wasn't all that alarmed, but then, in the afternoon, someone called and said he'd read the phone number on Buck's collar. A car had run him down not far from the hospital. Maybe he was on his way there to visit you, or maybe he thought you two should depart for the next world together. They told me his body had already been taken to the incinerator.

Only about five people came to your burial, the neighbours and a couple of old friends, ancient ladies still capable of locomotion. The priest spoke like the owner of a car dealership, using conventional, slightly tired language to extol the excellence of his wares.

The year was a few days from its end; as we left the cemetery, we were greeted by a burst of fireworks.

A noisy group of kids was on the bus. They must have had a lot to drink already; one of them was wearing a Santa hat, and another was masked like a skull with living eyes.

Once I was home, I did nothing but sleep. For three or four days, I slept heavily, dreamlessly. The house was cold, and the sudden gusts of wind made the shutters bang violently against the walls. Every now and then, that sharp, violent sound – it was like a gunshot – jolted me out of sleep.

After I started moving around again, the great absence I felt every day wasn't yours, but Buck's. I still talked to him, went looking for him, put leftovers aside for him. I was strongly tempted to go to the dog pound and choose a replacement, but then I became submerged under the infinite amount of paperwork required by the conclusion of a life.

I still couldn't feel any grief at your not being there.

The rooms were empty, immersed in silence like a theatre after the performance: no more shuffling, no more footsteps, no more coughing fits.

The part of me that should have abandoned itself to mourning had been prematurely used up, burned away by exasperation and by your brutally abrupt decline. I'd welcomed your passing with a feeling of relief, grateful that your sufferings were finally over.

Only the passage of time allowed your image to re-emerge in my memory, so that I could again see the person who had been so important in my life.

Once all the bureaucratic requirements had been dealt with, I didn't know what to do. Your illness had drained away all my energy; I could feel no grief, just immense dismay.

Who are you? I asked myself. What will you be when you grow up?

I didn't have the slightest idea.

The bora blew with extraordinary intensity all January long. It snowed a few times as well – the deer even invaded the garden, looking for shoots to eat.

I stayed curled up in the armchair in front of the fire, beside the table with our books (by then covered with dust), and I could hear your voice telling me the story of the Three Little Pigs and the Big Bad Wolf. "'I'll huff and I'll puff and I'll blow your house in," the wolf bellowed though the door.'

'No wolf can get in here,' you'd say to reassure me. 'This is a solid brick house, built not on sand but on the hard rock of the Carso.'

Then you'd add that foundations and roots are in a way the same thing, because they both make it possible to stand firm and not yield to the violence of the wind. In order to give a house stability, you have to dig deep foundations, down and down, just the way the roots of a tree do, year after year, in the darkness of the earth. In America, however – you went on – they set houses directly on the ground, like tents, and that was why a wolf's huffing and puffing would be enough to eradicate entire cities over there.

Alone in the silence of the house, I wasn't so sure about your words any more. I had the impression that the wind was hissing through fissures in the window frame, repeating *It's over, it's ooooover*, like when I was a little girl and the spinning washing machine would whisper, *Everything's useless, everything's doomed*.

In the middle of the night, the front door groaned under the blows of the bora; it really sounded as though someone were outside, shouting *Gestapo!*

By day, instead of protecting myself from the wind, I went out to confront it, running against its gusts like Don Quixote charging the windmills. *Kill me, purify me, ravish me, carry me far away, away from here, rip me out of my life*. In my heart, I ceaselessly repeated these words.

I slept little, I ate even less, I saw no one, I had no projects; I felt like a boxer alone in the middle of the ring. I'd warmed up for years, worked on my jab and my uppercut, and skipped rope to prepare myself for the final bout, and then my opponent had suddenly and unexpectedly withdrawn. I kept on hopping about, of course, but the only adversary I faced was my shadow.

Without any opportunities for conflict, my life was like a carrier bag at the mercy of the wind; my movements were determined by its capricious gusts, not by my own will.

I'd never thought about my future.

As a little girl, I'd had a few unfocused dreams about what I wanted to be – a stationmaster (complete with signal paddle and red cap) or a ship's captain, a circus acrobat or a dog trainer – but they were just that, only dreams, without any practical connection to reality. From the beginning of my teenage years on, I'd had but one occupation: attacking you. Now that you'd abandoned the field in one brilliant move, I walked around the house like Pavlov's dog, pulling at my chain and baring my teeth, but the bell I so longed to hear never rang.

What meaning did the days of my life have, now that I was alone in the world? Or, for that matter, even when you were still there? And, in general, what was the significance of all human life? Why did people always repeat the same gestures? Out of habit, out of boredom, out of an inability to imagine anything different or to question themselves? Or perhaps out of fear, because it's easier to follow a trail that's already marked.

Pushing my trolley down the aisles of the supermarket, I looked at the pallid faces under the neon lights and asked myself: What life has meaning? And what's the meaning of life? Eating? Surviving? Reproducing? Animals do all that, too. Then why do we have two legs to walk on and two hands to use? Why do we write poetry, paint pictures, compose symphonies? Only so our bellies can be full and we can copulate enough to guarantee ourselves descendants?

No human being desires to come into the world. One fine day, without being consulted, we find ourselves shoved out on to the stage; some of us are given leading roles, others are mere extras, and still others exit the scene before the end of the act or prefer to climb down from the stage and enjoy the show from the stalls – to laugh, weep, or grow bored, according to the day's programme.

In spite of this brutal start, once born into the world, no one wants to leave it. It seemed paradoxical to me: I don't ask to come here, but once I'm here, I don't ever want to leave. What's the meaning of individual responsibility, then? Am I the one who chooses, or am I chosen?

Is the real act of free will, therefore – the one that differentiates men from animals – the decision to leave for good? I didn't choose to come into the world, but I can choose when to bid it farewell; I didn't come down here of my own free will, but I can go back up whenever I want.

But come down from where? Go back up where? Is there an above and a below? Or just an absolute pneumatic void?

After your death, whenever I thought about the house, the image that came into my mind was the image of a seashell. When I was a little girl, not yet six years old, you bought me one from an old fisherman in Grado. I can still hear your voice as you put the shell over my ear and said, 'You hear that? It's the sound of the sea.'

I listened for a while, and then I suddenly burst into one of those intense, unstoppable fits of weeping that irritated and frightened you at the same time. You kept saying, 'Why are you crying? What's wrong?'

I couldn't answer you. I couldn't tell you that the sound inside the shell wasn't the roar of the sea but the groans of the dead, that the strange howling I heard was their voice. I couldn't say that it poured itself into our ears with all the violence of the unspoken, and that from there it went to the heart, crushing it until it exploded. Once upon a time, that seashell had housed a gastropod (just as, for many decades, the house on the Kras Plateau had been our family's protective shell) which some crab or starfish had then devoured, leaving its calcium carbonate exoskeleton empty. The water, entering every recess of the shell, had smoothed and polished it until it shone like mother-of-pearl, and now, deep in its gleaming insides, that sound reverberated endlessly.

The inhabitants of our house had undergone the same fate: They were all dead, and the wind had smoothed down every memory of them. Alone, I wandered through the chambers and spirals, and sometimes I seemed to be lost in a labyrinth. At other times, however, I realised that only by staying in there, only by searching and digging and listening, would I be able to find a way of anchoring myself.

The wind was a voice, too; it carried the sighs of the dead, the sound of their steps, the things that were never said between them.

As I was there alone, in that house whose walls kept getting thinner, more transparent, I began to think about the young woman in the photograph, enveloped in a cloud of smoke. I tried to remember the sound of her voice, the warmth of her hand, something that might have united us before she disappeared. I would have liked to know everything about her, but now there wasn't anyone I could ask.

How did she look, who was she, what did she like, and – perhaps the most pressing question of all – why did she bring me into the world?

I started calling out to her as I wandered through the empty rooms.

I was ashamed of speaking that name – somehow it seemed as though I were betraying you. Up until that day, I'd always said 'Grandma', and now, all at once, all I wanted to say was 'Mamma'.

Genealogies

6

Who are our parents? What's behind the faces of the people who begot us? Out of billions of persons, only two; out of hundreds of thousands of spermatozoa, only one. Before we become the children of our mother and father, we're the result of billions of combinations and choices – both made and not made – but no one's in a position to shed much light on them. Why that spermatozoon and not this one right next to it? Why does only *that* one contain the characteristics of the necessary person? The unborn child could turn out to be Leonardo da Vinci, or a plumber, or a ruthless murderer.

And if it's true that everything's already predetermined, as in a restaurant menu, if Leonardo has to become Leonardo and nobody else and the same with the plumber and the killer, what sense is there to our entire existence? Are we really just put together from various parts, like pieces in an assembly kit? Is there a number on each kit that determines the project it contains?

Maybe, up in heaven, someone – like an industrious housewife – is bustling about and deciding: Today we need four hundred plumbers, eighty or so murderers, and forty-two scientists.

Or maybe heaven's empty, as many people claim, and things go forward in a kind of perpetual motion; matter started to aggregate distant aeons ago, and now it can't stop; the forms it produces are more and more complex. And it's exactly this complexity that's opened the way to the great fiction that would have us believe in the existence of Someone up there in the sky.

Why can two people, a couple who perhaps hadn't even met until a few hours before, by performing an act that lasts no more than a few minutes, become our parents? Is this our destiny, to be half one and half the other, even if fate decrees that we're to be adopted and sent to live on the other side of the world?

In any case, we're part of them, and vice versa.

Part of them, and part of their parents and of their parents' parents, and so on, farther and farther back, until the whole family tree is covered – one grand-father's passion for insects, great-grandmother's love of singing, great-great-grandfather's flair for business, the other grandfather's alcoholism, various cousins' efforts to bring the family to ruin, the suicidal instincts of a couple of uncles, a great-aunt's obsession with the spirit world – all of that is closed up inside us as though in a time bomb. But we don't set the timer; it's been set from the beginning, and we know nothing about it. The only wisdom is to be aware that there's something uncontrolled inside us and that at any moment it could explode.

And so a man and a woman – among billions of their kind – meet each other at a certain point in their lives, and after a period of time that can vary from a few minutes to decades, reproduce themselves in another living individual.

According to the most advanced studies, the origin of this coupling probably can be found, once again, in the sense of smell, as is the case with migratory birds.

In fact, the human nose is the instrument through which we understand that the gametes of the person before us must be united with our own. There are no whys or wherefores, only the law of life, which seems to require that biological considerations trump all others.

It's the nose, therefore, that suggests copulation, because this extraordinary organ (a valuable legacy from our distant ancestors) never errs, and the only mood it knows is the imperative: Do this, do that, make sure your line will continue into the future, shining like a star.

So do we follow our nose, or fate?

Is the improvement of the species the main factor, or

is it the fragility of human beings, with their inexhaustible and inexplicable need for love?

The only image I have of my father in his youth – of the father I was able to track down after you died – is in a group photograph. He's standing behind my mother. They're holding cans of beer, as if they're making a toast – the occasion is a meeting or a party, it's hard to tell – and she's looking up at him with the devotion of a dog watching its master. The smoke from her cigarette mingles with the other smoke hanging in a pall over the room. On the back of the photo, a date in pencil: March 1970.

This photograph was one of many family pictures mingled together in a large cardboard suitcase, which I found in the attic, buried under a couple of carpets. I also found many letters, some of them bound together with ribbons of various colours, others tossed confusedly into plastic bags along with postcards from Salsomaggiore, from Cortina d'Ampezzo, from the earth pyramids in the South Tyrol, and from Porretta Terme, as well as train tickets, museum tickets, wedding invitations, birth announcements, messages of condolence, and, at the bottom of the suitcase, four or five notebooks, which, judging from their covers, dated from different periods.

In addition, for reasons only you could fathom, you

had saved two boxes of pins (one held safety pins and the other dress-making pins with coloured heads), a broken pair of scissors, an old caramel box containing buttons of every shape and size, an eraser, a tube of dried-up glue, a box of safety matches, a brochure from the Society of Dilettante Latinists, a train schedule from just after the war, a few recipes clipped out of newspapers, and a Bible whose cover had been removed by time, or mice.

Judging from the dust, that suitcase hadn't been opened for years; surely a good while had passed since your last venture into the attic, and I'd never even considered it. The desire to turn back and explore the past comes only when life changes for some unforeseen or terrible reason, such as an illness or a sudden void. Then, for example, a girl fetches a ladder and ratchets up her courage, because she needs to climb up and get all dusty and open the suitcase. And inside she finds repressed, unspoken words, deeds never done, and people never met; a tiny impact is all that's needed to liberate the ghosts.

The first ghost I came across wasn't my father's (although back then I wouldn't have been able to recognise him) but my mother's. I spotted it by surprise – it was hidden under a diary, a packet of letters, and a few scattered photographs.

I gathered up everything very carefully and went down to the living room. I didn't want to stay up in the attic, in *their* territory; I felt too vulnerable. By way of pretending that I wasn't alone, I switched on the television set and sat down in the armchair.

The pages of the diary were of Florentine paper with little lilies printed on it. On the first page, someone had drawn cubical letters in red ink with a felt-tipped pen: REBELLION. The word was underlined three times and followed by an indeterminate number of exclamation points.

14 September, 1969
Holy Cross Day
What's so uplifting about a cross? Bah! The only uplifting thing I can think of is that today's my first day of freedom! Farewell to the noxious exhalations of Trieste; farewell to the prison of my family.

Making her accept my choice wasn't easy. I could take the same courses in Trieste, so why incur the expense of moving to another city?

The Mummy gave in before I thought she would. The magic word was 'autonomy': 'I want to test my autonomy.' She lit up. 'If that's the reason,' she said, 'I'm in agreement.' I could have told her that I was going no matter what she said. I've finally stopped being a minor, and I can do whatever the hell I want. I've already lost two years because of her closed mind.

When I came here in July, an announcement on the

bulletin board at the university led me to this flat right away. It's a real hole. I'm sharing it with Tiziana, who comes from Comelico and is studying medicine.

In any case, I don't stay home very much. I feel like a dog who, after trying for many years, has finally managed to jump the fence; I'm always roaming around, sniffing the air, my eyes wide open in wonder, and I'm determined to try everything, to understand everything.

21 September
Back from buying groceries – they have to last for a whole week!

27 September
Half of what I bought has disappeared from the fridge. Asked T., who denies everything. Avoided an argument.

2 October
Telephone call from the M. I'm still asleep when the phone rings. She says the bora's blowing ferociously – it's cracked the trunk of a tree in the garden. 'Why would I care about that?' I say and hang up. I know very well that this is just one of her ways of controlling me.

13 October
First class. The lecture theatre's full, I get here late, and I have to stand the whole time. The professor's an

old guy with a reputation as a fascist. While he's speaking, there's a lot of tension in the air. Balls of wadded-up paper fly from one part of the hall to another. When, at the end, he explains the lecture schedule, a group of students rise to their feet and start hissing and whistling, joined by a large number of the others. The professor leaves in a huff, accompanied by a chorus of mocking laughter.

15 October
T. never buys groceries. She waits for me to do it so she can live like a parasite. She's selfish and stingy, and one of these days I'm going to tell her so.

30 October
The M. called, at dawn as usual – she must be convinced that being a student is like being a farmer. 'There's a long weekend coming up,' she said. 'Why don't you come home?' I was feeling magnanimous, so I said, 'Because I have to study.' Then I turned on to the other side of the bed and went back to sleep.

4 November
Today, when I woke up, I thought about the times we're living in. It's incredible. Everything's changing so insanely fast there's no more room for hypocrisy, conformism, or injustice. It's as if we've all suddenly opened our eyes

and understood that we can't go on in the old way. No more duplicity! No more slavery! The boss can't exploit the worker any more! The man can't exploit the woman! Religion can no longer oppress humankind.

Freedom is the operative word for the times to come. Freedom for workers, freedom for women, freedom for children – they don't have to be caged up in the obtuse rigidity of the educational system any more. We mustn't clip their wings, because a different world can arise only from spontaneity and freedom, and we, we ourselves, are going to be the protagonists of this revolutionary change!

18 November
I've begun my philosophy of language course. The teacher's an assistant professor. He's got only a few grey hairs, and they make him even more fascinating. He's the only professor who has a beard. Everyone listens to his lectures with great attention. When we left the lecture theatre, I said to Carla, my new study partner, 'Not a bad-looking guy, Professor Ancona.' C.'s smile was slightly malicious: 'You think you're the only one who's noticed that?'

2 December
C. managed to drag me to a women's consciousness-raising group. At first, I felt a little embarrassed, because they were all talking about their own bodies.

According to them, they had finally learned to know their bodies only because of the disintegration of the atavistic sense of guilt they had all shared, and this new knowledge allowed them to recognise the incredible violence that had been done to their imaginations with the childhood injunction that girls must play only with dolls and miniature cooking sets. 'The prelude to slavery!' one of the women shouted, and everyone applauded.

My turn was coming up, and I didn't know what to say. Then a memory came to me like a flash, an episode with my father: I must have been six or seven, and after dinner, walking with great care, I brought him his coffee in the living room. 'What a good little housewife!' he exclaimed, smiling at me.

Now, I said, it was clear that I'd been carrying that mark, that burden, that destination stamp inside me ever since. What if I'd wanted to become a neurosurgeon or an astronaut? My words caught everyone's attention and earned general agreement. To hell with the good little housewives and all other clippers of wings. When I left the meeting, I felt as though I'd grown lighter.

27 December
In order to keep the skirmishes from escalating into full-scale warfare, I had to come home for Christmas. On Christmas Eve, there was the usual gathering of

widowed friends, depressed women, and distant relatives with nowhere else to go, and that way at least we could all be together and feel so very very good.

The M., as usual, played the victim, announcing more than once that she'd been cooking for two entire days and hoping to receive applause and shouts of joy as her reward. And so it came to pass, as though according to a script. The comedy was played all the way through, right to the end, and no one missed a line. 'It's been a perfectly lovely evening, my dear, thanks so much,' kiss kiss, 'It was nothing, nothing at all, the bare minimum,' and so on and so forth, in a cloying minuet.

'Cloying' was also the word for the tree, with all its silvery tinsel, but nothing cloyed like the crèche: the ultimate representation of universal brainwashing, the Holy Family, which has been neutering normal families for two thousand years. There's nothing sacred about those other families, but they pretend all the same, drain their poisoned chalices to the dregs, and go forth with a smile.

That night in my bed, however, I thought about the Madonna, about how she's basically the symbol of the woman of bygone days, the most exploited of all, because she had a child without even getting to enjoy the sexual act; when she looked the Holy Spirit in the eye, that was enough, it was all over for her, and for nearly two *thousand years she's been standing around with that blank expression on her face.*

And so, in the morning, before I left, I did her a favour. I snatched the little statue from her place at St Joseph's side, left a note in the crèche that said 'get over it,' and took the Madonna out for some fresh air.

Before getting on the bus, I put the statue on the low wall behind the bus stop. Let's hope someone picks her up and carries her around for a while to help make up for lost time.

31 December
Seeing that T.'s still back in her snowbound valley, I'm giving a big party tonight. While I was shopping earlier, I ran into Professor A. My heart skipped a beat when I saw him. I would've liked to talk to him, but shyness overcame me. I thought he'd probably look at me with terror in his eyes – he can't be expected to remember all his students!

As I moved away from him, pushing my cart, I had the feeling he was looking at me. His eyes are black as coal, and when he speaks they seem to flash. Maybe they're the reason why I felt such intense heat right between my shoulder-blades.

Goodbye, old year; we'll bid you farewell, wrapped in the dense smoke of the peace pipe.

When 1969 came to an end, I closed the diary.

An anonymous car alarm sounded somewhere in the distance. There was a talk show on the television. Everyone talked and talked, with empty faces. The sheets on my bed were extraordinarily cold; no matter how tightly I curled myself up, I couldn't get warm. The light of the April moon came in through a crack in the closed shutters, slicing the floor and the desk in half and settling on Ilaria's photograph.

Despite all the things I'd imagined, dreamed, or conjectured about my mother, the simplest thing had never entered my mind: she was only a girl.

By nine the following morning, I was already in the living room. Before opening the diary, I put the photographs on the table in front of me as though they were cards in a game of solitaire: photos of her alone, photos of her with her girlfriends, photos taken by her, photos of members of the opposite sex. These last, however, were in the minority, and for the most part they were group shots.

Of all these photos, there was one that had been taken in a booth. It must have been winter, because she's wearing a scarf and a woollen beret in the picture. There's a male presence next to her, covering his face with one hand; in between his spread fingers, you can barely glimpse his eyes and a bit of his beard. Was it carnival time? Were they horsing around? What does that open hand represent? A rejection? A barrier? Maybe he was married and didn't want to compromise himself, or maybe he simply didn't like recording the fact that he maintained personal relationships with his female students.

I compared this photograph with the one where the group is making a toast. Besides the man with the beard, there's another guy standing next to my mother. This one's somewhat punier than the other, and his face is covered with acne. Farther to the right, crouched like a football player in front of a couple of girls – Carla? Tiziana? – there's a pale fellow with bulging blue eyes and a red scarf too tightly wound around his neck.

Might I be *his* daughter? Or the pimply guy's? The only one with a beard, in fact, is the man standing right behind her. I compared his hands to mine, his eyes to mine, and then I started reading again.

I progressed very cautiously through the pages, like a driver reading the warning signs – danger landslides, danger falling rocks, danger sheer cliffs – but not stopping, driving on with his foot hovering above the brake, his hand ready to downshift, his heart in his mouth, because that's the only road in the world he wants to follow all the way to the end.

6 January, 1970

The Twelfth Night fairy, that old witch, brought me a gift. Against my will, I was dragged to a party where I didn't know anyone, and there I met Professor A.

When I saw who it was, I kept my cool, or at least I tried to, but my cheeks were glowing all of a sudden, and so I turned towards the wall and started chatting with a woman I hardly knew, someone I'd glimpsed at a feminist group meeting, all the while thinking about how I was going to approach him.

Which turned out to be unnecessary, as he was the one who walked up to me. 'I have a feeling we've met before,' he said, searching my eyes while sipping slowly from his glass of red wine.

I think my voice came out unexpectedly shrill: 'Yes, at the supermarket!' I said (what an idiot), and then, fortunately, I added, 'I'm one of your students.'

He slipped his arm under mine. 'You're interested in philosophy?'

'Very much.'

After the party was over, we went for a walk under the porticos and kept going until we came to the irrigation ditches. Banks of fog were rising, and in the silence of the sleeping city, we could hear only the lapping of the water and the sound of our own breathing. By the time we crossed the piazza in front of the basilica, his arm was practically locked against my side. In the east, the sun began to rise, illuminating roofs and the façades of buildings.

'Look,' he said. 'Philosophy and the sun resemble each other. Both of them serve to chase away the night – physical night and the night of the mind – which oppresses human life with dark superstitions.'

We said goodnight at the main entrance to my building. 'Will we see each other again?' I asked him. He waved goodbye mysteriously with an open hand.

11 January
Unfortunately, I've started chewing my fingernails again. I looked for his name in the phone book, but there's no Massimo Ancona. I can't call him and I don't know where he lives. All I can do is wait.

15 January
I got to the lecture hall an hour early so I could sit in the front row, but he never looked at me, even though I was right in front of him. Maybe he didn't want to be distracted; he didn't want to give himself away in front of the others.

I waited for him at the door, but a red-headed guy was quicker than me. They went down the corridor together, talking as if they'd known each other a long time. Probably one of his final year students . . .

25 January

Two more useless classes. I think I'm going nuts. I've been going to the supermarket a lot, hoping to run into him. Nothing.

28 January

One carnival party after another, but I'm not having any fun at all. The women from the group dressed up like witches, but I went as a skeleton, because that's the way I feel without him, without a look from him: dead. I go to parties only in the hopes of finding him there. And then he's not, and I wind up smoking one joint after another. At least that makes the time pass more quickly . . .

30 January

I'd like to interrupt the class and scream in his face: Why won't you look at me any more? Last night I dreamed about doing it, and in the morning my jawbone was rigid like steel. Unburdened myself to C. She says my only problem is fear; her intuition tells her that the feeling between him and me is too big, too important, and that's why I'm afraid to go any further. I think she's right.

Why should I run away, when nothing has happened between us? C. advised me to make the first move. Times have changed. The days are gone when girls acted like pretty little statuettes in public and moaned in private.

2 February

Finally managed to leave a note in his mailbox in the professors' lounge. After thinking for a long time, I wrote, 'The light of intellect chases away the shadows of superstition. I'm free any night to wait for the dawn together.' Then, as a precaution, I signed it with my name and address.

6 February

Lost in the crowd in the lecture theatre. I think he started looking for me. I smiled at him, and it seems to me that he smiled, too.

12 February

Illusion, illusion, illusion . . . Maybe I should just give up and go back to Trieste and start all over again . . . or drown in clouds of smoke . . .

15 February

C. brought over some tabs. She said we could take a nice trip together, a voyage to an enchanted land, to worlds only we can see. I told her that at this particular moment, the only trip I have any desire to take is a trip inside Massimo's arms.

2 March

It happened! It happened! It happened! The magical

influence of spring? Who knows? And who gives a shit? The important thing is that it happened.

And I was so desolate, so worried! When he rang the doorbell, I was already in bed. I opened the door in my pyjamas (the ones with the teddy bears; not exactly a femme fatale outfit). I stammered, 'I'm sorry, I'm not . . .' His warm hands lightly touched my cheek. 'You're beautiful like this, too,' he said.

15 April
Maybe I was born just so I could experience the days I'm living through now. With him by my side, everything's changed. I feel like a giant; I'm freed from all my fears, all my urges to conform; my body has no more limits. Massimo has no fear of barriers – in fact, he seeks them out just in order to tear them down.

Two days at home for Easter: like landing on another planet.

The M. says, 'At last, your colour's good!' My complexion – that's what interests my mother. The outside, the mask.

If she were a different person, I could tell her all about my life now, but what can you tell a dead fish that spends its days in the freezer? Every now and then I think about them. I observed my parents closed up in the airless vacuum they lived in for years, and I saw that they had nothing to say to each other, they felt

nothing for each other, and I wonder how they ever
managed to conceive me. Am I really their daughter?
Do I look like them? Or not?

Maybe he was impotent; maybe they adopted me and
she doesn't have the nerve to tell me so. But what differ-
ence does that make? In the end, what's really impor-
tant is that I live a liberated life, without constraints
and without hypocrisy.

When I said goodbye, for the first time I almost felt
sorry for her, poor old mummy, all wrapped up in her
ragged bandages.

1 May
I'm not going to the demonstration because my head
is spinning. C. says I should take a pregnancy test.
In any case, according to her, I shouldn't worry,
because getting rid of it is a snap. The girls from the
group will see to it, and it won't cost me a single
lira. But she says I shouldn't wait too long; other-
wise, she says, I'll have to go to London, and every-
thing will get complicated. I feel strange, suspended,
speechless. I never thought anything like this would
happen.

3 May
Positive.

All at once, I jump to my feet; the pages and the photographs slide to the floor. I put on my anorak and go out for a long walk along the ridge of the Carso.

Down below, the sea glints like a mirror. Behind me, Mt Nanos is still covered with snow.

Positive.

It couldn't be me – the year isn't right. So what became of this sibling of mine?

The next day, the temperature is mild. Ever since dawn, all the birds have been singing together in a nonstop chorus, making a tremendous racket.

Compared to the warmth outdoors, the house seems like a dark, freezing cave. The diary's still on the table and the letters and photographs are still on the floor. In the darkness of the room, a yellowish light seems to emanate from them.

I take a deckchair from the garage and set it up in the garden, not far from the big plum tree, now completely covered with blossoms, which give off a delicate fragrance that attracts swarms of bees, including many bumblebees. Their frenzied buzzing keeps me company.

This is what I need so I can forge ahead: life, light, the sense that we're part of a much greater world.

12 May

I didn't have the nerve to go to class – I didn't have the nerve to look him in the eye. The way I feel changes every minute. Sometimes I think I'm carrying a lovely little secret around inside me. I want to take a long, romantic walk with him, and afterwards, maybe as we sip some wine, I want to whisper in his ear, 'You know what? We're going to have a baby,' and watch his reaction, which is first astonished and then delighted. Then, all too soon, the whole thing starts to seem like an unbearable burden, something that crushes me and won't let me breathe.

I'm afraid of the commitment, the effort, the responsibility; I wanted a life with no limits or barriers, and right away I shut myself up in the claustrophobic cage of motherhood. And what do I tell my mother? That I'm pregnant by a man nearly twenty years older than I am? I could invent some whopper, a romantic adventure in Turkey, seeing that Massimo smokes like a Turk . . . Or I could show up at the house with him one day and say, 'Mamma, this is the man I love, the man whose baby I'm expecting,' and I'd think to myself, our relationship will never be as dreary as yours.

Maybe he can't wait to introduce me to his family. Maybe, but it's useless to keep on fantasising. Before anything else, he has to hear the news; we can decide the rest together. Every time I see Carla, she asks me, 'Well?' as if to say I'd better hurry up.

20 May

He hasn't taken a class in two weeks. I've asked around, and it seems he's ill. By my reckoning, I'm at the end of my second month. The sweet euphoria is fading away more and more each day, replaced by fear and then anger. Is he really sick? Or has he perhaps guessed something and wants to take his time? I haven't heard from him in a month. Maybe he's really very sick, and it's only me, wicked me, imagining anything different.

24 May

Carla convened a special meeting of the group, because, she said, 'If we can't make decisions together, what the hell is sisterhood about?' I was a bit embarrassed at first – it seemed more like a trial than a meeting – but then the ice broke and a bunch of lovely things were said. For a while there were two parties, pro and con, but as the discussion went on, their positions grew less rigid.

P.'s the one who lit the fuse: 'First of all, before we can make a decision, we have to know whether the child would be a girl or a boy. We don't want to bring another enemy into the world.' Some members of the group applauded and others didn't.

B.'s reply was swift: 'In my opinion, if it's a boy, that's all the more reason to keep it. If we don't start turning out a new kind of man, who else will?'

More applause, and then a chorus of shouts: 'Yes, we'll make them play with kitchen sets! We'll make them coddle dolls! We'll teach them that aggressiveness isn't necessary! We'll make them wear yellow and red, no blue anywhere! And no princes, just children!'

'And let's not forget,' C. said in conclusion. 'Let's never forget nature, our teacher. Does a lioness ask her lion, "Sweetheart, do you want to keep this cub or not?" No! She has her cub and that's it, and then all the lionesses raise their cubs together, like a real sisterhood. Women and their young: this is the law that governs the world – all the rest is idle chatter. Males are useful for only a few instants – after that, they're no longer necessary.' The room exploded in roars of approval.

Waving my hand, I managed with some difficulty to make myself heard. I tried to tell the truth: 'Comrades! I . . . I don't know what to do . . . I don't know if I want to keep the baby.'

A great silence descended on the room.

'Whatever the decision is, you're the one who must make it. As your sisters, our only duty is to be here for you. If you want to keep it, we'll do what lionesses do and raise it together. If you want to terminate, we'll take care of that, too. L. and G. have taken a course and they've become very good.'

With these words, the official meeting broke up, and at last joints were extracted from handbags.

5 June

I went to the faculty office and asked for news.

'Professor Ancona won't begin lecturing again until next year,' I was told.

I had the presence of mind to say that I was one of his final year students and I absolutely had to talk to him. I might have blushed, however, because the secretary gave me a slightly suspicious look.

'Can't you consult with his substitute?'

'Oh, no . . .'

'Then write him a letter and give it to us here in the office.'

The subsequent pages of the diary were covered with scratched-out sentences, probably repeated attempts to find the right words. Every now and then, through the thick scrawl of the felt-tipped pen, some fragment appeared like a fish escaped from a net. *Love* squirted out on one page, and *responsibility* on the next. *What to do? Keep b.* emerges, and under it, written three times in capital letters with many underlines: *DESPERATE, DESPERATE, DESPERATE.*

Before she wrote the letter, she must have made many foul copies – after all, he was a professor of philosophy, specialising in the philosophy of language. As I read those fragments, I got the impression that she was terrified of using the wrong words; every sentence betrayed the great insecurity with which it was written. She seemed like a person suffering from vertigo and forced to walk along the edge of a cliff. The precipice was a choice: life or death.

While she was attending meetings or anxiously hurrying to class, while she was smoking or (probably) weeping in her bed, that brother or sister of mine kept taking shape in her body. With immense sagacity and an imperturbable rhythm, the cells were multiplying and arranging themselves to form what would have been its face one day. The baby was growing inside her, and she couldn't decide whether to let it be born or not; her power over it was total. As I read those lines, I couldn't feel any hostility or contempt toward her. My only instinct was to protect her, as if all her desperation, her solitude, and her laughable naivety had gone directly into my veins, coalescing into a sense of infinite pity.

By this time, the midday sun was unbearably hot; it even stunned the insects buzzing around the flowers. Just when I was about to close the diary, a bumblebee fell on the pages, its rear legs covered with pollen. Delicately, I helped it get airborne again.

On the spot where the bee had fallen, there was a sort of golden halo. I read the lines below it:

It's decided.
Three days from today, at B.'s house.

From the heights of her medical studies, Tiziana said, 'You're crazy. They'll kill you.'

I replied, 'Maybe that would be even better.'

After this, two pages have been torn out. Then, with a nervous hand, she wrote these lines:

The night afterwards, suspended between relief and confusion, I had a dream. I'm not sure where I was in the dream – all I remember is that at one point I ate a piece of unbaked bread dough, which started to rise in my stomach. Everyone I came across said, 'Are you expecting?' 'No,' I replied, 'It's just the yeast, still working,' but when I said that, I wasn't so convinced I was right any more.

When I woke up, I felt strange, so I called B. 'Are you sure everything went OK?' I asked her. She reassured me; the procedure had been perfectly executed. 'Besides,' she added, 'I showed it to you in the basin, remember?'

She seemed vaguely offended at my having doubted her abilities, so to lighten things up, I made a joke: 'But suppose you did what the Filipino healers do and showed me a couple of chicken livers?' We laughed, and the tension was relieved.

I felt I needed to extract myself from my mother's life for a few days. I couldn't bear the heaviness of those years any longer.

In order to get rid of the dross and the shadows, in order to purify myself, I took several long hikes across the plateau. Hidden in the bushes, the blackbirds and the blackcaps mingled their love songs, and the tender green of the recently-sprouted leaves lent splendour to the surrounding landscape. A giant cloud of busy pollinators buzzed above the upland meadows, which were dotted with dandelions, daisies, and crocuses.

Sometimes I stretched out in the damp depths of a sinkhole. From where I lay, I could admire the crown of bushes and trees around the rim, while backlit spiders climbed up and down invisible strands of silk, and beetles like violet jewels rumbled heavily through the air. At other times, however, I felt the need to climb higher, to reach a point from which I could gaze out to the far horizon and beyond.

As I walked between the sinkholes and the heights along the Slovenian border, I thought about my brother – or my sister – who was denied the possibility of being born. Would the child's existence have saved my mother, or would it have accelerated her self-destructive decline? Would I be in the world, I wondered, if that older sibling had been here? Was his or her end also, somehow, the possibility of my beginning?

Beyond our will, our fragility, and our plans, however circumscribed, is there Someone or something that governs the great cycle of births? Why was

I born, and not the other one? The abortion could have failed, just as my mother could have lost me involuntarily, perhaps by tripping on the stairs with me inside her.

I ascended and descended the stony paths. As I passed, the grass snakes basking in the sun shook off their lethargy and whished away into the bushes. Wall lizards darted here and there. When a snake comes into the world, I said to myself, or a harvest mouse or a crow, none of them can distinguish itself from the rest of its kind except by its longevity, its ability to stay alive. An animal (for all its extraordinary complexity) can only carry out, more or less effectively, the project inscribed in the genetic patrimony of its species, but what about man? Can't a human being change the path he's on, again and again? And isn't it this bottomless chasm of potential that dismays us, that suggests the impotence of our vision? Who would my brother have been? And as for me, why have I come into the world? Who am I supposed to become?

Those long walks gave me the strength to continue my researches. One morning, I woke to the clicking sound of raindrops against the windowpane. The dark bora, the *bora scura*, had come up in the night, the temperature had dropped, and the wind was blowing pretty hard, covering the garden in an autumnal light. The innumerable white petals scattered under the plum and cherry trees were the only reminders that spring had begun.

After a bit of breakfast, I slowly climbed back up into the attic. An old curtain in a floral pattern covered a pile of boxes, large and small. Some of them must have once contained liqueurs and chocolates; others were anonymous cardboard boxes sealed with packing tape. With the aid of a penknife, I opened one of them, which turned out to be full of Christmas decorations. I unwound several metres of silver ribbon before I got to the crèche. The stable wasn't old or particularly well made: two cork walls and a ladder leading up to a kind of hayloft under the roof. Inside, the ox and the ass lay with their legs sticking up in the air, while St Joseph and the Madonna rested on their sides. A small bag contained the manger, the sheep, and the lambs. I found my favourite little statue: an old plaster ewe with one broken limb and a red ribbon around her neck. She was the one I used to hide every Christmas Eve; she was the little lost sheep I made you look for, bleating through all the rooms of the house.

There was no trace of Baby Jesus. He must have been in another box, or maybe he wound up in somebody's pocket during Advent. I also discovered the few glass baubles that had managed to survive decades of Christmases and a treetop ornament with a hole in it.

The boxes underneath held Grandfather's various beetle collections: little glass cases with velvet lining, to which the insects were affixed with long, slender pins, the whole labelled with each insect's Latin name, written out in a clear, unhesitating hand.

While I was cautiously trying to move the cases to one side, I tripped over a plastic bag, sealed with electrical tape and bearing the insignia of the State Police; inside there seemed to be a cloth shoulder bag. For a few moments, my heart accelerated its pace. What could it be if not the purse my mother had with her at the time of the accident?

I tore through the plastic wrapping with my fingernails. The bag had no zippers, just a single button, undone. Inside I found a wallet with a few thousand lire, a membership card for an alternative film club, a few dinars, a train pass for the Trieste–Padua stretch, and, protected inside a transparent envelope, a faded Polaroid snapshot of me as a baby at the seashore, in the arms of a man. The stranger – his hair long and dishevelled, a shell necklace around his neck – smiles at the camera, but I'm clearly irritated. I've got a little bucket in my hand, and either I've just finished crying or I'm about to start. From what I can see in the background, we must be at Sistiana Bay.

In addition to the wallet, there was a ballpoint pen with dried-up ink, a packet of cigarette papers, a little rolling machine, house keys, a synthetic-fabric scarf, a lipstick, some smokers' sweets, and, hidden in an interior pocket, two letters. The first, addressed to my mother, had been sent from Padua a few months before I was born.

The handwriting was tiny and regular, with a touch of angularity in the strokes.

Dear Ilaria,

I've received your letter and I'm responding to it at once because I don't want you to waste your time waiting in vain and I don't want to encourage illusions that will only make you miserable.

If I were just a bit more hypocritical, if the times weren't what they are – and naked-truth-telling therefore not so thoroughly de rigueur – I could lie to you and tell you I'm married and that I have no intention of endangering my marriage for the sake of a one-month affair.

Instead, I prefer to be honest and tell you clearly that I don't want any children. Not any children, or any wives, or any fiancées, or anything that might limit my freedom in any way whatsoever. I don't want any of that, because I lead a life of exploration, and explorers can't travel with ballast.

I gather from your words – which are sometimes (pardon me) rather too saccharine – that you don't feel that way, that you're still harbouring grand illusions. Moreover, even though several years have passed since we first met, you're still very young, and the distillate of bourgeois respectability (and sentimentality) that you absorbed in your formative years is still intact. Despite your progressive opinions, all you really aspire to is a popular-song vision of life – two hearts and a cabin – perhaps in its revolutionary version: 'You and I and our offspring, marching into the bright future.'

'We'll build a different world,' you write. 'It's up to us to give the example of a new kind of relationship, without oppression, without exploitation, without violence. Raising children creatively, living as a liberated couple.'

In your opinion, in short, we should play at being young pioneers, and you're convinced that in this way you'll succeed – we'll succeed – in freeing ourselves from the obtuse destiny of the bourgeois, from that long death agony which marriage has always been for everyone.

Only your guilelessness makes me feel indulgent towards you. Besides – why deny it? – it's the part of you I've always liked the most, right from the first moment we met. For this reason, and by virtue of our brief time together, I feel it's my duty to offer you a few points to reflect upon.

The word 'love' occurs several times in your text. Have you ever asked yourself what's hiding behind that noun, so often used and so often abused? Has it ever occurred to you to consider that love may be a sort of scenery, a cardboard backdrop whose purpose is to give the performance some ambience? The chief characteristic of backdrops is that they change with every change of scene.

The essence of dramaturgy doesn't lie in that painted cardboard — the visual illusion helps us to dream, to consider the pill a little less bitter — but if we're honest with ourselves, we can't deny that we're face to face with a simple artifice, a fiction.

Love, which has so generously nourished your fantasies, is nothing but a subtle form of poison. It acts slowly but inexorably, and it's capable of destroying any life with its invisible emanations.

You'll get that lost look in your eyes and ask, 'Why?' Because in order to love a person, you must first know him. Can the complexity of one human being truly know the complexity of another? The answer is obviously, absolutely No. Therefore, really loving someone is impossible because really knowing him isn't possible.

You've come to know a tiny fraction of me, just as I've been able to enter into contact with a tiny fraction of you. We offered each other, reciprocally, the best part of ourselves, the one each of us knew the other wouldn't be able to resist.

The same thing happens with flowers. To attract the

pollinator, the corolla exhibits extraordinary colours, but once the act is completed, the petals fall, and little is left of the flower's former splendour.

There's nothing shocking about this — it's a law of nature. All couplings occur as a result of various forms of seduction. Every species, from flowers to humans, has its own ways. But just as the bee can't say 'I love you' to the flower, so too are we unable to lie through our teeth and say we love each other. In these honest, forthright times, the only thing we can properly say (as the bee says to the flower and vice versa) is, 'You're necessary to me'.

Years ago, in a difficult moment of my life, I felt the necessity of immersing myself in freshness for a month or two. At the same time, I was necessary to you, too — at least, I hope so — as a means of opening your eyes to some complex questions. And of course, there was the undeniable pleasure our bodies gave each other. And pleasure — beyond the orgasmic enjoyment itself — is also extraordinarily subversive. Meeting you again after a few years confirmed our bodies' magnificent mutual attraction.

What I've said up to this point logically applies to the arrival of a child as well. The flowers that let themselves be fecundated by pollen surely don't do it for pleasure; they do it to assure the survival of their kind, to guarantee that other flowers like them will exist in the future.

The same mechanism is innate in human beings as

well. Despite the complexity of our minds, our bodies want only to reproduce themselves. To them, as to the flowers, it makes no difference whatsoever whether we love each other or not, or how overwhelming the orgasm was. A birth can just as easily be the result of a rape, or of a premature ejaculation. Out of two hundred and fifty thousand spermatozoa, there's only ever one that wins the race – the best, the strongest, the luckiest, the most dishonest – it makes no difference. What matters is that life is replicated and passed on. And that's what happened in your case, too. It's a law of nature.

To tell you the truth, I ought to slap your wrists a little. Why didn't you take some preventative measures? I know you're dreamy and romantic, but do you still believe in baby delivery by stork? Or maybe what you desired, not so unconsciously, but clearly, wilfully, was a connection, a link that would bind me to you once and for all?

Probably, given the depth and the archaic nature of your conditioning, and even though you don't realise it, what you (like so many of your female friends) truly want is only the certainty of a future as part of a couple. Some men, faced with women's biological and primeval blackmail, lower their guard and yield. They do it because they're weak or banal or afflicted by the innate and unconquerable fear of death. Who but their child can guarantee them eternity?

Many yield, but not I. Any vacillation I might indulge

*in is blocked by the idea that the baby growing inside you
will be not only a stranger, but also a tyrant capable of
consuming the energy of our days, a parasite capable of
devouring – without any sense of guilt – the people who
brought it into the world. I would never be able to know it
and therefore never able to love it. You won't be able to
either, despite your having carried it in your womb. One
morning you'll wake up with a realisation: you've brought
an interloper into the house, and that interloper has the
face of an enemy.*

    *All that having been said, I don't want to influence
you in any way. As you and your friends chant in your
marches, 'My womb is mine, I'll manage it myself'.
Do what you want. If you want to keep it, keep it; if
you want an abortion, I have no objection. Either
decision leaves me completely indifferent.*

    *Just remember, if you appear in front of me one day
with a bundle in your arms, I won't be even slightly
moved, nor will I betray my convictions.*

    *I'm grateful to you for the lovely hours we spent
together, for the philosophy, the poetry, the sex, and for
the guilelessness that was always in your eyes when you
looked at me.*

    M.

My father and the father of my dead sibling were, therefore, one and the same person. The same vile person.

By now, I had very few doubts about the contents of the other envelope, the white one. I opened it a little, peered in, and recognised the handwriting I'd come to know very well.

Every one of your words corroborated what I've always known. Children belong only to their mothers; after the fathers perform the necessary fertilisation, they are no longer required.

And soon they won't even be necessary any more; a donor and a syringe will be enough, and thus the pathetic history of the family, the ballet of make-believe that has destroyed the mental equilibrium of so many generations, will finally draw to a close.

Many of us live in my house in Trieste. I won't lack assistance or company. The child will grow up without blinkers and without hypocrisy. He'll never feel compelled to put up a poster in his room with the words, 'The family is airy and stimulating, like a gas chamber.'

He'll be a free child, and he'll be on the way to an equally free world, with no more mistaken ideas and without the repression imposed by patriarchy, capitalism, and the church.

He won't suffer from fears and anxiety, because his childhood will have been spent in accordance with the innate goodness closed up inside every human heart. And his soul will be so large that I may never truly learn to know it, but, unlike you, I'm not distressed by this prospect, nor will it make me go back on my decision.

That's the challenge: to send creatures more complete than ourselves out into the world. If we can't make a revolution with weapons, at least we can do it by raising our kids differently.

G. says that somewhere in the heavens it was written that you and I would meet, and that our existences would unite in a new life. Our destinies and the destiny of our child were inscribed in an astral conjunction long ago – I believe that, even though you won't accept it. Probably, in order to carry out this plan, we've been chasing each other through several lives, and since you refuse to procreate, your karma will be long and devastating. You'll probably be reincarnated in an animal; I can just see you as a reptile (your cold blood irrigating every cell of your body and its minuscule brain), or maybe a mandrill, with a bright red muzzle to match your behind.

Inevitably, your child will look like you; he'll have your eyes, your hands, and your way of laughing, but to me he'll be only himself, and you'll be an outdated mail-order catalogue. If he asks me anything about you, I'll tell him of a magnificent, impossible love shared one night on a distant beach . . . I'll make him dream about his father.

Luckily, I have G. in my life. I don't know what I

would have done without him. Despite your sarcasm, he's not my new lover; he's a unique person who's very important to me. All the broken pieces I'm carrying around inside – he's helping me put all that back together. He alone has the patience to make sense of every fragment and return it to its proper place. G. knows how to see things others don't see. He knows how to untangle the confused strands of people's lives and find the thread that will lead them to safety.

I've never told you this, but I was pregnant with your child a few years ago, too. You never learned about him, because he was no bigger than a tadpole when he got flushed down a toilet. I did everything by myself, without consulting anyone. At the moment, it seemed like an event of little importance; only now, as I'm digging through the ruins, do I realise how profoundly that act destabilised the whole edifice. In all likelihood, given the shoddy materials that had gone into its construction, it was pretty shaky already: behind me were my mother, with her bourgeois obtuseness, and my father, a grey man who sprinkled me with merely luke-warm affection, which I returned at an even lower temperature. He was a Coleopteron among the Coleoptera, like the metamorphosed cockroach in the story, taking refuge under the bed.

But I don't want to bore you with these bourgeois trivialities.

That first time, I threw away our child because I was afraid. Afraid of responsibility, of commitment, of having to give up my youth, of not being ready to work for the revolution; afraid of not measuring up in your eyes, of disappointing you. I lied to you the first time we slept together: I wasn't on the pill. And maybe one reason I had the abortion was that I was afraid you'd deride me for lying.

But the last few times, when we saw each other again after all those years, you never asked me anything about birth control. Do you know why? According to G., the answer is clear: you, too, however unconsciously, want a child. You're doing your Herod number to mask your terror, but at this point, I no longer have any interest in your fears. My belly's growing every day, and it's as though I have a little sun shining inside me. It's warm, it gives light, and it helps me to see my way forward.

I'll carry this pregnancy to term. I'm thirty years old and I can't wait any longer. I'm not the naive girl you portray in your letter, infatuated with her handsome professor – not any more. I'm an adult capable of making responsible choices, and I choose to be a mother. I don't have a job, but I've got a house in Trieste (a gift from my bourgeois family which I was careful not to reject). I spend a lot of time working on my unconscious, by no means a simple task. And from time to time I manage to do some tutoring. When my mother passes on to the next world, however, I'll have a stable income, so you needn't worry – you're going to be spared the spectacle of my coming to you begging with a baby in my arms. It won't ever happen.

Do you know what G. says? He says each of us is holding one end of a string, and that string can lead us to our star. Each of us has a star; our destiny is to learn how to follow it as it moves across the heavens. It's a kite-star, our karma is written in its wake, and if we let the string go, all is lost, everything gets tangled into a skein of stars.

In fact, that's the title of his most important book: Skeins of Stars. *I know you don't care about any of this, but believe me, if you don't seek out your star, if you don't follow it, sooner or later your string will snarl and snag with the strings leading to other stars, and there will be no untangling it; your star will grow dimmer and dimmer, until eventually it disappears altogether.*

The star's a little sun, but when its light fades, it becomes cold and icy. And that's the frigid gloom that will guide your steps while my child and I run happily along, following the rainbow of our kite-stars.

Om Shanti, Om Shanti, Om Shanti.

For a moment, while I was reading, a thick veil fell over my eyes; the words danced before them in agitation, and my hands weren't all that steady, either.

My mother's dreams didn't coincide with my memories in any way. What she thought of as freedom had caused me, child that I was, nothing but bewilderment and confusion. There was never any happy running after the rainbow. Her star was a star of destruction; the modest efforts she made to save herself had thrown me into a state of profound and lasting turmoil.

I put the two letters back into the inside pocket of the shoulder bag, handling them as delicately as archaeological finds newly come to light after centuries of burial. Rest in peace, I told them, rest in peace, white-hot darts, don't perforate my fragile guts.

As I was saying this, my hands grazed a folded sheet of graph paper lying at the bottom of the bag. The sheet had been torn clumsily from a notepad. What period did this fresh discovery date from?

The heading indicated that the page had been written in May of the year she died. Below the date, printed in block capitals, were the words YOU'VE MADE A FOOL OF ME ALL MY LIFE!

On the back of the page was a brief letter:

Forgive me, forgive me for bringing you into the world. I've made one mistake after another. I've spent my life burrowing underground like a mole, blind to everything, and running in circles like a mouse.

There was no horizon, and no future.

I was born to live in a dead end, and now I've run out of road.

Forgive me if you can.

If you can't, I understand. Hugs and kisses.

She'd cancelled her signature – *Ilaria* – with two thick black strokes, and then, just below that, she'd written in big, slightly childish letters, *Mamma*.

When your heart breaks, what sound does it make? A splat, like a waterlogged sponge, or a hiss, like a fire in the rain?

I would have liked to learn more, but that was all there was. I had nothing else to rely on but my memories, those few, weak flashes that belonged to the earliest period of my consciousness, but that door had been closed for too many years. My life – the life I knew – had belonged to you, to your house; everything that happened before I came to live here had dissolved. It was as though I'd been born at the age of four.

But going over those years again, discovering things about my mother that some children might never want to know about theirs, had stripped away a veil from my memory, as people returning home after a long absence pull the protective cloths from their sofas.

The first thing that came back to me was an extremely precise odour, the smell of cigarette tobacco and hashish burning in an airless room. Had I been a migratory bird, I could have followed that scent right back to the nest. The nest, in this case, was my mother's flat in Trieste, a sort of commune where people continuously came and went. I crawled around among men and women, some of them seated, others stretched out on the floor, forming alleyways I slipped through as though they were paths in a labyrinth.

I found only two snapshots from that period in the suitcase. In the first one, I'm in my mother's arms, dirty-faced, pouting, wearing a red sweater, and she – with long hair and bags under her eyes – is holding one of my hands and waving it, trying to make me say bye-bye to someone. The second photo was taken on my third birthday. There are a lot of people sitting on the floor, and I'm in the midst of them, and before me is a dark, shapeless mass, lit by three little candles, which must be the birthday cake. Behind me, a length of unrolled toilet paper is hanging like a banner, and someone has written 'Happy Birthday' on it with a felt-tipped pen.

I didn't have any real memory of those two events; what remained from the first years of my life was a kind of background noise, a soundtrack made up of competing voices and indeterminate racket, overlaid from time to time by the heartbreaking music of an instrument (later identified as a sitar) that made me cry.

I was afraid of that sound, I was afraid of being alone after everyone fell asleep on the floor, and I was afraid of the moment when the sun would be high in the sky and I'd shake my mother but instead of opening her eyes she'd turn over on her other side and keep on sleeping.

I was afraid of the sitar, and I was afraid of my mother, because often she wasn't herself; she was another person who snatched things and broke them, beat her head against the wall, and kicked doors.

Maybe it was that terror that cancelled her face from my memory. At any second, I knew that reality could blow up, explode into a thousand pieces, and somehow the lighting of the fuse had something to do with me.

Apart from the dismay and the constant anxiety of those days, I remember also the birth of something smaller and more devastating when it comes from a young child: the feeling of pity. Yes, pity was the knot in my throat that made me weep when she was lying exhausted on the floor and I'd move closer to her, fearfully and delicately, so that I could reach out and touch her face.

7

Could I continue to ignore my father the way he'd done me? This was the question I kept asking myself, but I found no reply.

During my teenage years, I'd fantasised a lot about him. I stopped believing your whopper about the Turkish prince (and also in Father Christmas) when I was nine, but I often thought about my father; day after day, I put together my personal mosaic of him. To accomplish this task, I used tesserae of the most extraordinary colours: the fact that he'd never tried to contact me must mean that some obstacle had prevented him from doing so, some impediment so dire that getting in touch with me would threaten his very existence, or maybe even my own.

Why else would a father deliberately choose not to watch his daughter grow up? Increasingly fantastic scenarios succeeded one another in my imagination; their settings extended from the venues of international espionage (only a spy would be unwilling to risk revealing his identity) to the most advanced scientific research laboratories (my father must be a biologist, physicist, or chemist working on projects of extraordinary significance for the future of mankind, and therefore he's compelled to live some sort of high-security underground existence, far from prying eyes, and to deny himself his daughter's love).

Children want to be proud of their parents; it's too bad that parents don't notice. In the most fortunate cases, a father and mother have an idea of how a child ought to be, and everything they say and do conforms to that idea. In the most unfortunate cases, the parents see nothing outside themselves, and they live their lives without noticing the laser beams constantly pointed at them, their child's wall-penetrating, distance-overcoming eyes, implacable, parched, hungry, capable of reaching them anywhere on earth, of following them to heaven or hell, ready to risk everything, to lose everything, eyes that have sought but one thing ever since they opened onto the world: an answering look.

Every child is born with a need for wonder; he wants to turn his eyes on something he can admire, to be led to a mountaintop where he can contemplate the splendid view, the changing light, the snow, the reflections on the ice, and the soaring eagle, majestically protecting its young, as human parents ought to do, too.

But instead, the landscape that stretches out before many children, all the way to the horizon, is often nothing but an open-air rubbish dump, where automobile carcasses, broken chairs, boilers, sinks, dead television sets, and plastic bags litter the ground: a single expanse of desolation and disorder. And nevertheless, even in such a situation, a child can manage to find something to admire – a marble, perhaps – and for a fraction of a second, as he holds the little glass sphere, the world contains no more shadows and shines in his hands.

To keep away despair, the child holds on to anything at all – a hint, an inkling – that he hopes may grow and broaden until it transforms the whole scene. There's not a detective or a scientist who can match the investigative talent of a child bent on finding valid reasons to admire the people who have brought him into the world.

A drunken father (let's say he's lying on the floor and you have to step over him on your way to school) isn't a bad person, not at all; he could have come home in a rage and started kicking you, but instead he chose to go to sleep and leave you in peace. And your mother's good, too, because after neglecting you for days, she comes home and makes you an omelette; she could have skipped that, she could have shut herself up in her room, especially since she's not hungry and so what if you are, but no, she takes out some eggs, beats them in a bowl, and maybe even looks you in the eye and asks you if you've done your homework, because you're the most important thing in her life.

For years, I'd enclosed my father in an imaginary bubble that followed me everywhere. The bubble was suspended in mid-air, and there he was inside, surrounded by flower petals, smiling the Buddha's peaceful smile: sublime, inaccessible. I was convinced that sooner or later, the bubble would burst and he'd finally descend to earth so he could put his arms around me.

The bubble did indeed burst; however, instead of the seraphic, imperturbable Buddha, out stepped Professor Ancona, with his beard, his cigarettes, and his words, reasonable on the surface but underneath as sharp as stilettos.

In those days of complete solitude, I read and reread his only letter to my mother. At first, I thought I might agree with some of what he wrote – about his love of knowledge, for example, or his decision to avoid personal ties in order to give himself over as utterly as possible to self-examination: this is a great mind, I told myself, so of course he has the right to avoid tying himself down, to keep himself free from quotidian concerns. But

I was still caught up in the bubble syndrome; I wanted to find in him something that was in me, too.

When I went over the letter again a few days later, it made a very different impression on me. It was as though a chemical reaction had taken place between the lines, and the measured, well-ordered, authoritative words now exuded a greenish, acidic, corrosive substance capable of bringing to light the true nature of the person who'd written them. I could see paternalism, derision, cynicism. My mother was portrayed as a character in some romantic novel, seduced and abandoned at her first encounter. The terms were different, of course, as well as the details, but 'scratch the surface' (as he used to say) and the story was always the same: The woman falls in love – and dreams – while the man plays a game and enjoys himself.

I'd fantasised for years about meeting my father for the first time, about our first embrace, but those few pages swept away any tender feeling or admiration from my heart and left behind only anger. I felt humiliated as a woman, as my mother's daughter (and therefore his, too), the product of degeneration rather than generation, brought into the world by a joke of fate.

Now I knew I'd spit on him the moment I saw him. I'd go looking for him, indeed I would, but not out of affection or curiosity, I'd do it only so I could vent the rage I felt rising inside me, so I could get close enough to him to shout into his ears all the things my mother should have said if she'd only had the nerve.

One thing was certain (and I took solace from it): despite his passion for freedom and his lofty opinion of himself, he'd never become what he'd hoped to be; otherwise, I would have read his name somewhere. He must have remained a small or medium-sized fish, shut up for life in the little protected aquarium provided by the university and a few specialised journals. My hunch was confirmed in a bookstore a few days later. On the title page of a book on epistemology translated from English, I read these words: 'Afterword by Professor Massimo Ancona'.

It wasn't hard to track him down. I called up his publishing house and asked for his address. They told me most politely that – for reasons of privacy – they weren't authorised to give out his address, but that I could write him a letter care of the house and they'd be sure to forward it to him.

So I took pen and paper and wrote to him. I presented myself as a philosophy student, young, shy, and filled with admiration for the fascinating complexity of his work.

Could we meet?

The reply wasn't long in coming. He didn't live very

far from Trieste. He thanked me, fended off my compliments, and added that there was no use in my making an appointment with him, because he was at home every afternoon except on Sundays. All I had to do was ring his bell downstairs and speak my name – Elena – into the intercom, and he'd buzz me in.

The first name I'd chosen for myself was Elena. For my family name, I used your mother's maiden name. I didn't want to run the slightest risk of arousing even a tiny suspicion and having our meeting cancelled.

And so the 'student' Elena, on a cold day with the bora blowing, took a bus to Grado to meet her father for the first time. She was on her way like Red Riding Hood's wolf, like Hop o' my Thumb's ogre, like all those fairytale creatures capable of biting and causing pain. But she was also going like a child, in naive anticipation, hoping that the story had taken a different turn with the passage of time, because that imaginary embrace was always there, waiting, the arms spread out inside her like the claws of a giant crab.

What was I feeling in the half-empty bus that carried me toward the seacoast, as I prepared myself for this meeting?

Was I fearful? Was I angry? Angry, for sure, but probably more afraid than anything. I watched a landscape of monotonous desolation roll by outside my little window. Soon after passing the cranes rising from the shipyards in Monfalcone, we began to cross over the estuary of the Isonzo River. Every now and then, the slow flight of a heron traversed the sky. Maybe I was more fearful than anything else because – after giving the matter so much thought and devising so many elaborate strategies of attack – I was no longer sure I'd have the nerve to push the button on the intercom or the strength to climb the stairs or the courage to meet his eyes without betraying my emotions, like Ulysses upon his return to Ithaca, shortly before he massacred the Suitors.

When we reached the stop I wanted, I was the only person who got off the bus. An elderly bicyclist pedalled toward me rather unsteadily from some distance down the deserted street.

Despite the name of the place – Grado Pineta, the pinewood of Grado – there were really very few pines to be seen, most of them pretty bare-looking and imprisoned in a grid of dilapidated blocks of flats with poetically evocative names: The Sirens, Seahorse, Star of the Sea, Nausicaa.

Over the course of the long winter months, the various little gardens had accumulated all sorts of bottles, waste paper, beer cans, and miscellaneous rubbish blown there by the wind.

In the days of the economic boom, this was a fashion-

able location for a second home; now the entire neigh-
borhood seemed like a galleon set adrift. For some time,
the salinity in the seawater had been busy about its work
of corroding plaster and wood, particularly door and
window frames. Many shutters hung askew; some rolling
blinds had collapsed. A crooked sign, riddled with holes,
was posted in front of a crumbling cottage: 'Villa
Luisella'. During the winter, apparently, someone had
amused himself by firing bullets at the sign. In the yard,
which I could see through the gate, a bicycle with only
one rim lay on its side.

I couldn't imagine how Professor Ancona had wound
up in a backwater like this. After a few vain attempts, I
finally managed to find the right street and the right
address: 18 via del Maestrale. Before me, in silhouette,
rose a building no less spectral than all the others, distin-
guished only by a little portico where it looked as though
people set up stalls in the summer (I imagined their
wares: inflatable dinghies and soccer balls, sun lotion
and beach chairs, lots of little buckets and spades); now,
however, the shops were empty, and I could look through
the dismal security shutters and see the empty counters,
the layer of dust on everything, the newspaper pages
scattered across the floor.

Massimo Ancona. It was one of the few names on the
intercom panel. I couldn't hesitate any longer; my doubt
was growing with each passing second. And out of that

doubt, there arose the overwhelming certainty that it would be better – for my life as well as his – if I were to turn on my heel and plunge back into the darkness from which I had come.

'Elena,' I said to the intercom.

'Fifth floor.'

I pushed the glass door open; as I entered the atrium, I spotted an orange and white life preserver hanging on the wall (in case these flats go under?) and printed with the name of the building: 'The Naiads'. I took the lift; then a door opened, and I found myself face to face with my father.

8

A closed-up odour – the smell of cold smoke – and semi-darkness. White furniture in summerhouse-on-the-beach style, doors falling off cabinets and wardrobes, laminated surfaces swollen by humidity. Books everywhere, scattered pages, on the floor an old typewriter under its dust cover, an open laptop – the single light source in the room – newspapers, magazines, a bottle of whisky standing next to a glass so smeared and smudged as to be nearly opaque, and a dirty quilt laid over a child's bed transformed into a sofa.

And in the middle of the room, him.

Same face as in the snapshot, just a little fuller; black hair, salt-and-pepper beard, burning eyes. His upper body was still slender, but sagging slightly because of his paunch, which pressed so hard against his shirt that the buttons seemed about to burst.

'What a lovely surprise on an otherwise melancholy afternoon!'

'I'm Elena, pleased to meet you,' I said. Then I sat down on the rickety sofa-bed.

After holding forth (and remaining duly vague) for a short while on the subject of myself and my studies, I gave him the floor. Which seemed to be just what he was waiting for. It occurred to me that he must be a very solitary man, his head always full of thoughts, and he leapt at the chance to address an audience.

My anger had given way to curiosity. I tried to see him through my mother's eyes: what had struck her about him? What emotions had he stirred in her, emotions with the power to determine her fate so tragically?

I tuned into his long monologue. 'You must be surprised,' he was saying, 'that I've chosen to live in such a shocking place. Perhaps you would have preferred to visit me in Venice, in a renovated loft above what was once a fishmonger's, with antique furniture and old prints on the walls, but that, you see, would have been too conventional. It would have meant adhering to a pre-established type – the philosophy professor in his natural habitat – and that's exactly what I don't want to do: step into a mould. Besides, there's something about cutting all ties; it's like setting up outposts in the void. I'm going where no one else would ever have the nerve to go, and do you know why? Because I'm not afraid. That's all there is to it. Since I don't live the lie of attachment to anything or anyone, I have no fear. It's duplicity that makes us fragile. We have to build around us a wall of things, of objects and simulacra, to hold terror at bay, but all this accumulation, instead of providing relief, generates an even greater terror, the terror of loss. The more attachments we have, the more we live in panic; things get lost or break, people die or leave us, and suddenly we find ourselves completely naked. Naked and desperate. Of course, we've always been naked, but we pretend not to know it, not to see it, and by the time we realise it, it's often too late for us to save ourselves. You may be wondering how a person can save himself if he can't hold on to anything. He saves himself by not acting – or rather by acting in harmony with the void. The void precedes us; the void will close in again after our brief passage. In the void there's a sort of wisdom, the wisdom of appearing and disappearing, and therefore we must entrust ourselves to the void as to a generous wet-nurse . . . *Outposts in the Void* is actually the title of the book I'm working on . . .'

Time passed, and I couldn't manage to step into the flowing river of his sentences. I still had an hour before the last bus. I didn't know how to approach the object of my visit.

Luckily, after a while he got up to refill his whisky

glass, and my eye fell on an extremely beautiful Persian rug, the only antique in the house.

I pointed to it and asked, 'So where did that come from?'

'Does it seem like a contradiction to you? It is, in fact. My father was a rug merchant – it's one of the few I still have.'

'Is it an heirloom?'

'No, it's my strongbox. Something I can sell if I have to . . .'

Instead of returning to his chair, he sat beside me on the sofa-bed. Its springs squeaked under his weight. We stayed like that for a while in silence; not far away, a dog was barking desperately. Then he took one of my hands and began examining it. 'According to the ancients, a person's hand contains all the qualities of his soul . . . Here I see intelligence and nobility of thought . . . Your hand is a lot like mine.'

Our hands were resting on my leg, side by side. Mine shook a little.

'It's a lot like yours because I'm your daughter,' I said, in a voice whose calmness amazed me.

The curses of an old man who was trying unsuccessfully to silence the dog overlaid its barking.

The professor sprang away from me. 'What's this, a joke?' he asked, in a voice halfway between alarm and amusement. 'Or a bit of bad theatre?'

'Padua, the seventies. One of your students . . .'

He stood up so he could see my face better. 'Marvellous years. Girls flung themselves into my arms like bees diving into a flower.'

'Naked-truth-telling.'

A hard light came into his eyes, rendering them opaque and extinguishing their bright flashes. 'If you're here to make accusations, let me tell you at once that you've come to the wrong place.'

'No accusations.'

'Then what do you want? Some compensation, some money? If that's the reason, the most I can give you is a rug.'

'I don't need money, and I don't want a rug.'

'Then why, assuming that you really are my daughter, have you come all the way out here?'

'Simple curiosity. I wanted to get to know you.'

'Human beings can never completely know each other.'

'But curiosity is an attribute of intelligence.'

'*Touché!*'

The bus would be passing very soon. While I was putting on my jacket, he opened the front door and said, 'Come back whenever you want. I'm always here in the afternoon. I often go out in the morning, so if you're going to come then it's best to call first.'

After that first time, I visited him once a week for three months. We often took walks along the beach. In the beginning, the bathing season was still far off, and on sunny days the strong-smelling clumps of algae rotting in the shallows along the shore attracted flocks of herring gulls, which were always on the lookout for food.

The water level varied greatly, in accordance with the tides. Sometimes, the fishermen-pensioners had to wade out almost to the horizon in order to find clams and scallops.

We frequently came across joggers, athletic young men or older, big-bellied fellows, dripping with sweat even in the middle of winter.

Often, during the milder days, we saw lovers sitting on the trunks of trees blown down by sea storms. On one such occasion, my father pointed to a couple locked in an embrace and said, 'Do you know why lovers love to look at the sea? It's because they're convinced that their love is without end, like the horizon. In short, they gaze at an illusory line and superimpose on it an illusory sentiment.'

He missed no opportunity to demonstrate to me the speciousness of the visible world. Maya – the great cosmic illusion, according to Indian Vedic philosophy – imprisons us in its magic net, from which only a select few manage to escape by finally opening their eyes. All the others are compelled to follow shadows.

'Love can't be only a shadow,' I replied.

'Of course it can. It's the shadow of partiality. Look, right now I'm glad to be walking with you along this beach, I like talking to you about a great many things, but is this love? No, it's only the satisfaction of partial knowledge. In you, who claim to be my daughter, I love the reflection of my intelligence; I love what I recognise of myself in you. But if, for example, you had displayed a different genetic trait – maybe something you shared with some dull-witted aunt on your side of the family or mine – if you'd turned out to be a silly girl living for talk shows and the latest style in trousers, I would have shown you the door at once. I'd even have changed my telephone number so you couldn't get in touch with me again. I'm not much interested in ownership – I much prefer recognition. I like the idea of detecting a sign, a trace, mysteriously passed on from generation to generation. And that's the reason – my aversion to ownership – why I let you be free. Try to imagine what your life would have been like if you had known from the start that you were Professor Ancona's daughter. You would have automatically conformed to pre-defined behavioural modules; for example, you might have felt duty-bound to be the first in your class. Or maybe you would have gone the other way and done your best to be as moronic as possible, putting nails through your eyelids and following every sort of repulsive fad like a sheep, just to drive me crazy with rage. But this way, you're not a product of conditioning, you've grown up naturally, and you've become what you should be, not a greenhouse plant but a tree, standing majestically alone in the middle of a clearing, and all that's thanks to me, because I hid myself from you, I withdrew. Don't think it wasn't a sacrifice on my part, as well. I had to renounce the innumerable little moments of delight granted only to fathers, but I didn't want to clip your wings. Do you understand? I preferred to let your genetic inheritance manifest itself on its own, without distortions or conditioning, because in the end that's our essence. For millennia, our DNA has rolled itself out, carrying in its strands the secret of how long our bodies can survive. You live, you survive, you die; everything's inscribed there, in that speck of matter.'

The sun was hot that day. We sat on a rowboat that had been hauled up on to the beach and took off our jackets. My father lit a cigarette. My eyes fell on a dead cormorant not far from us; some raptor must have eaten its head, and the flies swarmed around its gaping neck. Had I moved it, I'm sure I'd have found the maggots already at their work.

He'd never asked me anything about my mother, neither who she was – which one out of so many – nor what had become of her. This seemed strange to me.

'My mother's dead,' I said, without looking him in the face.

'Ah, yes?'

'She died a long time ago. I was four.'

'This, too, is a species of good fortune. How did she die?'

'In a car accident. I don't know much about it. I think everything had become too much for her, and somehow . . .'

The smoke from his cigarette rose in symmetrical rings and drifted in front of his face. He breathed a deep sigh. 'Right, that's how it goes,' he said. 'The gene for guile-lessness often carries a certain flaw.'

'What flaw?'

'A tendency toward self-destruction.'

One day, after our walk, he took me to lunch in the old town. He was probably a regular customer at the restaurant we went to, because the elderly waiter who led us to our table called him 'Professor'.

As we sat down, he whispered 'They're going to think you're my latest conquest.'

I wanted to say, 'Since when do you care about what other people think?' But I kept my mouth shut.

On the wall behind him, a drunk in an oil painting gave me the eye. There was an empty bottle on his table, his cap sat on his head at a jaunty angle, and two tears were running down his cheeks. In the painting beside it, an enormous orange sun shone down on two horses standing muzzle to muzzle and hoof to hoof, whether for rivalry or love was not clear. After all, my father would have said, they're the same thing.

'You should order the *brodetto con la polenta*,' he suggested.

'No, I'd rather have the fried calamari.'

While we waited, they brought us some antipasti and a bottle of white wine. It was the first time I'd ever seen him eat. I figured he'd treat his food, like everything else, with sovereign detachment; to my great surprise, however, he devoured everything greedily, with lowered head and swift fingers, as though he'd been fasting for a while.

Until then, he'd never asked me to tell him anything about myself and my life. Seeing him bent over his plate, I felt a well-grounded suspicion that it would have made no difference if I had been a mannequin or a cardboard cutout; things would have been exactly the same. But I wanted to know some things about him, and so, during our long wait for the main course, I interrogated him on the subject of his family.

His mother came from the island of Rhodes, and his father, Bruno Ancona, was a rug dealer. Actually, he'd graduated from the university with a degree in Business Economics, but then he'd inherited the rug business from his father-in-law. Faced with the choice between working for an insurance company and travelling all over the East, looking for the best pieces, he opted for the rugs. They lived in Venice, where my father was born in 1932.

Shortly before the Racial Laws were enacted in 1938, Bruno Ancona and his family, along with a chest full of rugs, boarded a ship bound for Brazil. Bruno's wife, Massimo's mother, had opposed this move with all her might, the meetings of her canasta club were regular and well-attended, all the ladies were still playing, and there was no reason for alarm.

They were Italians. Italians like everyone else.

Throughout the entire crossing, Bruno had to put up with his wife's complaining. 'You've got too much imagination,' she kept telling him. 'Your imagination's dragging us down to ruin.'

Her torment continued uninterrupted even after they reached São Paolo. Everything was too much for her; the city was too damp, too hot, too dirty, too poor, too full of blacks, and what was worse, there was no one to play canasta with. She held out for two more years, and then she got sick and died.

'A stupid woman, on the whole' was my father's comment. 'Very beautiful, with olive skin and eyes like burning coals, but stupid.'

Bruno, on the other hand, wasn't stupid at all; a year after becoming a widower, he got married again. His new wife was a dark-skinned Brazilian beauty, who produced a string of coloured kids.

After the war, Massimo had asked his father for his inheritance and returned to Europe. He'd never seen nor heard from him again; he didn't even know whether he was dead or alive.

'That's not important, either,' he concluded, avidly sucking the claw of some crustacean. 'The past can't be changed, and the future doesn't belong to us. What really exists is the present. The moment, and nothing else, is what's important.'

When I went back to Trieste that evening, the odour of fried food accompanied me all the way home. I was tired and all I wanted to do was sleep, but I had to take a shower first. I was afraid that dreary smell would get inside me somehow and mingle with my sadness.

9

The following week, I didn't go to visit him.

His speeches had settled on my thoughts like dust on furniture, slipping into the cracks and the empty spaces and making everything dim; it wasn't the innocent dirt caused by neglect, the kind you can get rid of at once with a cloth or a lungful of air, but a fine, mephitic powder, capable of concealing among its molecules some dangerous metals or metalloids like lead and arsenic, substances which, absorbed in small doses, cause no symptoms at first, but which later, with the passage of time, lead to poisoning and death.

On many occasions, as he talked, I'd found myself agreeing with his words: after all, I shared his scorn for appearances and for sentimental fictions. The obtuseness I caught a glimpse of in many people's faces irritated and terrorised me at the same time. What life could there be behind those opaque eyes? Such an existence would surely never be mine, but what was the alternative to opacity? Thanks to his temperament (which was also my own), my father had followed a different drummer, but was his life really free?

The image he loved to project, his metaphor for himself, was that of a solitary tree, standing alone in the midst of a clearing, lifting its majestic branches to the sky.

But didn't his life instead resemble one of those massive plane trees that line urban avenues, heedless of pissing dogs and the waste paper and cigarette butts and tin cans accumulated among its roots, indifferent to the fluorescent spray lovers use to record their names on its trunk, unconcerned by the increasingly vile obscenities carved into its bark?

A tree whose roots can't breathe, suffocated by asphalt as they are, a tree with greyish leaves and a soot-blackened trunk, a tree exhausted by the vibrations of passing buses, which nevertheless, in spite of everything, maintains its lofty elevation, because like all trees it desires one thing and one thing only: to drink the light. And in order to do so, it must keep growing taller and taller, until it rises past the shadows of the surrounding buildings. Every winter, the Municipal Department of Parks and Recreation cancels out this hard-won victory, polling and pruning until nothing is left of the beautiful branches but tiny stumps. Despite such mutilation, however, the plane tree doesn't give up; every spring, new shoots arise from its amputated arms and then, from those tender twigs, the first leaves.

It hurts the heart to see a tree reduced to such circumstances, especially if you know how much space it can take up in a clearing. Many of those who don't have any idea gush in admiration all the same: 'Look how beautiful it is!' says the grandfather to his grandson. 'It's putting out leaves!'

It never occurs to the old fellow that the haggard apparition before him is the result of a death agony protracted over decades, the song of a dying whale riddled with harpoons and sinking into the sea.

When I was with my father, I felt like a rabbit in a python's coils; the complexity and boldness of his reasoning took my breath away, made my head spin.

But as soon as I was out of his presence, I thought over what he had said, and then my dizziness turned to impatience, and the image of the plane tree kept recurring in my mind. My father had sought the truth with the same force that drives the tree yearning upward towards the light, but in doing so he rejected life, and in the end all he could do was wrap around himself. He was like a wanderer waiting at a bus stop in the desert, unaware of how many years it's been since that line was in service.

What would have happened, for example, if he'd accepted his share of the responsibility for my mother's pregnancy instead of washing his hands of the entire affair, if he'd married her, if he'd maintained his relationships with his father and the other members of his family, and if he'd kept his teaching post at the university and dedicated himself with passionate energy to the formation of his students?

In short, what would his life – and the lives of those around him – have been like had he accepted his responsibilities instead of running away from them?

What's the relationship between truth and life?

That was the crucial question, the one I repeated to myself over and over during the course of those months. I pondered over it for his sake but also for my own.

Nights were the worst.

Alone in that big house, exasperated by the sound of the wind as it banged the shutters, I was certain that with the passage of time my father's search for the truth had turned into a big screen, like one of those handsome, handmade, artfully embroidered Chinese screens, but always mounted against a background of heavy cloth, a barrier he could hide behind.

When my thoughts turned to my mother, my anger changed into rage. If she was so guileless, so naive, why abandon her to her fate? Didn't he feel any remorse? Was I really just the result of a biochemical reaction between two agents otherwise unconnected to each other? Had the March light, by stimulating the hypothalamus and triggering a hormonal storm, compelled my parents' coupling, whereupon their fluids mingled and that was that?

The same thing happens with toads. In February, they meet in ponds, and in March they go back to the woods, leaving their eggs behind them. But a toad never asks himself: Who am I? Does my life have any meaning?

Was my mother a toad, a porcupine, a grass snake, or was she something different, something in any case unrepeatable? And was her death attributable only to an innate inability to survive in the jungle of life, or were other people partly responsible? Were actions not taken, things not done – or done badly – by those closest to her, whose duty it was to help her, given that they were older and more experienced than she was?

Is it really possible to compare animals to humans?

More than once, in the heart of the night, tangled inextricably in the web of these ratiocinations, I grabbed the telephone, ready to shout in his ear, 'You disgust me! I hate you! Go to hell!' But every time, I entered the dialling code and stopped, overcome by an inexplicable fear.

Was I afraid, perhaps, of his mocking voice, of his

inevitable crowing, 'I knew it would end like this'? Or did I fear falling – with no right of appeal – into the mucilaginous mass to which he contemptuously relegated 'other people'? Other people, normal people, the ones who make the best of their situation, who have neither the intelligence nor the guts to get to their feet and scan the horizon; all the wretches who march in the quotidian parade, banging away like bass drummers, never noticing that life has no meaning.

Normal people like my mother, like his father (with his dark-skinned wife and mulatto kids), like the students who couldn't stand up to him, like the friends (if he ever had any) or the women who didn't have the nerve to follow him to his outposts in the void.

And yes, to be honest, my hesitation was also caused by fear of his contempt; I wasn't ready to undergo any sort of humiliation from him. After all (at least this is what I believed at the time), he was the only relative I had in the world, the person closest to me by blood. For better or worse, I owed fifty per cent of my genes to him.

In those months, I started focusing on the details of what we had in common; the more closely I looked, the more I saw. That's the reason, I thought, why I can't bring myself to break off our relationship so abruptly. When the time is right, I'll go to his house and enumerate for him, calmly and clearly, the reasons for my contempt.

I told myself I'd be the one who'd decide to break it off with him, and not vice versa. The last thing I wanted was to wind up like my mother, abandoned along the way like a suitcase with a broken handle.

By the time high summer arrived, all the tribulations of that year – your sickness, your death, meeting my father – had taken their toll on me, and I was as limp and worn out as an old rag. The only thing I wanted to do was to stay by myself, sprawled somewhere, without food, without words, regaining my strength like a plant in winter, or like a marmot waiting for the snow to thaw.

It had been three weeks since my last visit to Grado.

Late one afternoon, the telephone rang. It was him. His voice sounded different – what had happened to all that mocking aloofness? – as he lodged his complaint: 'What's the matter? You're not coming here any more?'

Almost without realising it, I tried to justify myself. 'I'm not feeling very well. As soon as I'm better, I'll come.'

Why didn't I have the presence of mind to say, 'I'll come when it suits me,' or, better yet, 'if it suits me'? Why did I let myself feel guilty about a person I'd seen maybe ten times, a man who'd never himself felt, I won't say a sense of guilt, but not even the faintest twinge of remorse, a seducer who'd always behaved as though none of his actions would ever have any consequences?

I didn't go to Grado the next week or the week after that, even though I was feeling better, nor did I call him. Then the telephone rang at the same time three afternoons in a row, but I didn't even dream of extending my hand and picking up the handset. Evidently, he was looking for me, without any success. I derived some covert satisfaction from the thought of his anxiety.

On the fourth day, I answered.

He began the conversation with 'Is that you?'

There was a hesitation bordering on fear in his voice; he sounded like an old man. Maybe he was a little drunk, because his tone quavered and lurched like a candle flame in a draft.

I was waiting for him to say something to me, to ask how I was doing or whether I was over my illness, but instead, after a heavy sigh, he said, 'I can't stay here any more. The whole place has turned into a madhouse. It's full of crying babies and screaming television sets, the stairs have been invaded by fat women wielding ladles, the men are DIY fanatics with drills and weed whackers; instead of assaulting their wives, they assault their neighbours' nerves. Do you know what my outpost has turned into? The launching pad for a miniature apocalypse. Every year it's the same thing, or rather, every year it gets worse. Fortunately, during the summer a friend of mine lets me use his flat in Busto Arsizio, so that becomes my summer outpost. I'm leaving to go there now, but I wanted to give you the address, just in case . . .'

'What?'

'Just in case you should feel like paying a visit. I can give you a telephone number, too. Do you have something to write with?'

'Yes,' I replied, scribbling the number on the back of an old receipt.

'But remember to let it ring three times, hang up, and then call again. Otherwise, I won't answer. I try to stay out of most people's reach.'

'I know.'

'Listen . . .' His voice took on a fragile note that was almost unsettling. 'I wanted to tell you something else . . .'

'Yes?'

He was interrupted by children's voices, shouting ferociously over the sound of rap music suddenly turned to full volume. 'I'll tell you another time,' he said. 'I can't take it any longer . . . I've got to get away!'

Thus, with a reference to flight – his preferred activity – he hung up.

When he came out with that 'I want to tell you something else,' my heart beat faster; I expected a revelation, an admission, a memory, a sign of contrition, something that would point our relationship in a normal human direction, something that would authorise me to stop calling him Massimo and start calling him Papa.

It's possible he merely wanted to notify me that he was going away, and wasn't that very act a first step along the way to capitulation? I'm telling you where I'm going to be because I need you, because I'm waiting for your visit, because I can no longer live without hearing your voice, without seeing your face?

After the phone call, I went out into the garden.

The air was saturated with ozone, and the swift, menacing clouds of a big storm were rolling in from the east, still some way off, but already torn by flashes of lightning that lit up the horizon. A dry wind – which precedes storms – shook the sparse crowns of the black pines and made their branches crackle before swooping down on the golden fruit of the plum tree. The plums fell to earth with the thudding splat of bodies filled with water. In the opposite direction, the sun was already vanishing from the sky, and the light that normal terrestrial rotation had so far spared was swallowed up by the onrushing clouds.

Soon the storm would burst over the upland plain, but in my heart and mind it had already begun, it had knocked down power lines, and electricity was running everywhere, like a sprite dancing for joy.

10

When an aeroplane crashes, the first thing people look for is the black box; apparently, the same goes for trains. Everything is recorded in that small space, including all the factors that contributed, however minimally, to the accident – speed, trajectory, human error, indecision, darkness, and so forth – right up to the moment of impact. In people, the equivalent processes are entrusted to the power of recollection. Memory constructs human beings, situating them in their own personal history as well as in that of the world around them, and words are the traces we leave behind.

Words are like the footprints you find on a beach at dawn. During the night, a great multitude of creatures has come and gone among the dunes: foxes, mice, rooks, seagulls, deer, boars, sandpipers, crabs, and also those little black beetles that scamper and dash along the sand like ladies who are forever late. They all pass this way in the darkness and leave their tracks. Some of them meet and sniff one another curiously; others land and then take off again; the least fortunate are devoured, while still others mate or simply stretch their limbs. Crabs build sandcastles as they burrow into the beach. Sandpipers' tracks last until the next wave wipes them out. The little black beetles leave long, orderly trails behind them on the sand, making it easy to retrace their steps to their lair.

And you, what lair did you emerge from? And where are you going?

However, before asking ourselves where we're going, we ought to discover where we've come from.

If the beetle doesn't know what species he belongs to, how can he behave properly? How can he know whether he's supposed to eat dung, pollen, or dead animals?

An animal knows what it was nourished on in the long, drowsy time of its first consciousness; the remembered taste of that food guides it in its choices, and it's likewise able to recognise its lair and the compelling reason for leaving it. Everything is inscribed in its genes.

In humans, on the other hand, things are more complicated.

We're alike in our physical functions, but extremely different in all the rest. Every one of us has a history that's his alone, and its roots go back very far, to grandparents, great-grandparents, great-great-grandparents, and beyond, farther and farther back, until they come to the first man, to the moment when — instead of behaving like beetles — we began to make choices.

What choices did our ancestors make? What burdens did they hand down to us? And why does the weight of those burdens vary so much? Why do some of us stride forth, feather-light, while others can't manage a single step?

With these thoughts in my head, I climbed back up into the attic. The summer sun had begun to heat the trapped air, and I opened the little window to keep from suffocating. I sat with my legs crossed beside the open suitcase on the floor. There wasn't very much left in it: some dusty, ageing letters and a small notebook that looked more recent, all of them abandoned like confetti after a carnival celebration. These were the last traces, the ripples in the sand left by the beetle before it reached its lair.

Where would those pages carry me?

I was afraid of being disappointed. Maybe this stuff was just a collection of trite missives sent by my great-grandparents from one thermal spa or other: 'The treatments are having an effect . . . the food's good . . . we'll be back Thursday on the eight o'clock train.'

I carried the letters and notebook downstairs, put them

on the table, and arranged them by date, but by then it was late; I didn't feel like opening them when there was nothing left of the day but its dark edge. I decided to wait for the light of the following morning.

After I went to bed, the music of some summer festival disturbed me, and I couldn't go to sleep. Around one in the morning, when I looked at the alarm clock, the air was resounding with the strains of the leftist song 'Bandiera rossa'. Only at three a.m. did silence finally descend on the plateau, broken by the occasional roar of a lorry. I could hear in the distance, although weakly, the twanging of the shrouds on the sailing boats anchored in the harbour. They seemed to be performing a little concerto in the gentle breezes of a light summer bora.

What music is that, I wondered, dozing off at last: the symphony of departure, or the symphony of return?

On the cover of the notebook, a wintry landscape. In the foreground, rabbit tracks across the snow; in the centre, a stand of trees, their branches laden and white; in the background, closing the horizon under a clear, luminous sky, a mountain range glistening with ice. It was a simple notebook, the kind you'd use for Latin exercises or household accounts. Maybe that's why I opened it carelessly.

But I froze, all carelessness gone, as soon as I recognised my mother's handwriting.

One word was written on the first page: *Poems*. I'd perused her diary and read her letter to my father without any sense of embarrassment, but now, with that note-book in front of me, I felt upset and intimidated; I'd never imagined that my mother had a poetic side.

There were several compositions – some of them short, others quite long. I leafed through the notebook, stopping to read a poem here and there.

I'll Never Be a Flower

I'll never be a flower
that offers its corolla to the sun in spring.
I'll never be a flower
because my spirit is more like the grass,
a thin blade equal to a thousand others,
as tall as the others, bowing its head
at the first winter frost.

Fog

The fog wraps up everything, houses and people;
even bicycles stop making noise.
Our world is a world of ghosts
or am I the ghost?
My heart is wrapped up in cotton wool
a precious gift
addressed to no one.

Fear

It's not monsters that frighten me
nor is it murderers.
I'm not afraid of the dark
or of floods or cataclysms
or punishment or death
or a love that doesn't exist.
I'm afraid only
of your little hand
groping for mine,
of your gentle gaze
looking up at me and asking, 'Why?'

My vision blurred; I felt something pressing on the centre of my breastbone. It seemed like a pole of some kind, one of those sharpened stakes used to kill vampires. A hand was thrusting it at me forcefully, trying to split open my rib cage.

It Would Have Been Lovely

How lovely it would have been
had our life been as happy
as a Sanremo Festival song.
You and I, hand in hand,
and on the windowsill a box of lilacs.
How lovely it would have been

to wait for sunset together
and not to fear the night.
How lovely it would have been
to guide our children's footsteps
with a single hand.
But the ogre came and devoured
the little time we had
leaving only bones and peels on the ground,
the remnants of his obscene feast.

The stake thrust deeper, penetrating my diaphragm; had it turned a bit to the left, it would have perforated my pericardium.

Was this woman my mother? What happened to the troubled, superficial girl of the diary, the confused, desperate woman of the letter? She must have written those poems shortly before she died, but in any case they seemed to record the thoughts of a different person.

I've heard it said that when the end is near, everything becomes clearer; it happens even if we don't know our days are numbered. All of a sudden, a veil is torn away and we see clearly what has, until that moment, remained in darkness.

My mother was entirely a product of her time. She let herself be ferried along by the generational current, never suspecting how close she was to plunging into the abyss. Since she'd grown up without solid roots, the violence of the rapids bowled her over. She wasn't like a willow, which can be overwhelmed by a flood and still stand its ground; she truly was a humble blade of grass, as she wrote in her poem. The little clod of earth she stood on was swept over the precipice, committing her to solitary navigation. Maybe it was only when she heard the roar of the waterfall, only when she was about to be hurled into the unknown, that she regretted those roots she'd never had.

After all, I thought, the way people are put together isn't very different from the limestone landscape of the Kras: on the surface, days, months, years, centuries of history in continual transformation succeed one another – carriages or cars pass over it, simple day trippers, defeated armies – while, underneath, its life remains intact and ever the same. There are no fluctuations of light or temperature in its dark caverns, no seasons or changes; the olms splash about happily, rain or shine, and the stalactites keep descending toward the stalagmites, like lovers separated by some perverse divinity. In that water-created world, everything lives and repeats itself in a nearly immutable order.

So in the years of revolution, my mother had lived an ardent life. In order to subscribe to that dream, she'd distorted her own feelings. At the time, they weren't as important as the approval of the group.

Packed together on the prow of an imaginary

icebreaker, they moved forward, breaking the obtuse, frozen crust, their eyes fixed on the luminous horizon of universal justice. If the ship could keep moving, they'd finally reach a new world, a land in which evil would have no more reason to exist and brotherhood would reign supreme. The magnitude of this task permitted no vacillation and no indecision. They had to go forward united, without individualism and without regrets, marching to a single rhythm, like the African ants that can devour an elephant in a few minutes.

At a certain point, however, she must have distanced herself from the group in some way. While many of her companions were literally taking up arms, my mother chose the solitary path of introspection. She was drowning, too fragile and confused to save herself, and then she came across this Mr G., the first buoy she could cling to. He held her up and helped her float, and that must have been more than enough for her. For a little while, the skein of stars allowed her to go on, while patriarchy and capitalism camouflaged the unresolved karmic bonds.

But in reality, below that surface appearance, beneath the hard ideological bark and the confused aspiration towards some abstract universal harmony, there was a young woman who nevertheless, in the most hidden part of her being, dreamed of love.

The river kept flowing in the deep caverns, and its

water was the real source of life, with its power to slake, nourish, fertilise, strengthen, and unite human beings in every corner of the earth. But it's loving and being loved, not revolution, that's the innermost aspiration of every creature that comes into the world.

11

Many factors cause disease in trees, and even more contribute to the maladies that afflict human beings.

When its sickness has advanced too far, a tree's chances of survival are slim. Its roots rot, its trunk swells, its metabolic processes are interrupted, and its leaves, starved of sap, fall to the ground.

When a person falls ill, viruses or bacteria are the usual suspects, and justifiably so, but no one asks where they came from, how did they happen to creep inside there, why today and not a month ago, and why this person and not that other, who may well have been much more exposed to the risk of a contagion? When two patients receive the same treatment, why does one recover and the other succumb?

A lightning bolt grazing the bark of an ancient oak can suffice to initiate the process that leads to its destruction:

bacteria, funguses, and beetles enter the breach and propagate rapidly, and soon the tree is in peril of its life.

Fruit trees become fragile when they lose their verticality. Even if the wind bends a pine, it can keep growing, but a bent apricot tree cannot; its exact perpendicularity to the ground is what allows the tree to live and bear fruit.

To destroy a human being, to make him sick, what's required? And what's needed to heal him? What's the significance of an illness in the course of a life? Damnation? Bad luck? Or perhaps an unexpected opportunity, a precious gift from heaven?

When someone's ill, isn't his lamp turned on?

During the long weeks I spent in the hospital, the image of the lamp kept returning to my mind. I saw myself as a fairytale gnome, lantern in hand, trying to explore an unknown space. I didn't know where I was going. With fearful steps, I skulked among the robust roots of a centuries-old tree or crept down a mole's burrow or made my way through the labyrinth of a pyramid. I moved forward cautiously, frightened but also impatient. I guessed that sooner or later I'd come to an unknown door, and the closer I got, the clearer it became that through that door I'd find the treasure. Like the open door Aladdin finds, this one would lead to a room where chests filled with pearls and precious stones and gold ingots were stored and waiting, just for me. I didn't know who had hidden them there or what his motives had been; my sole desire was to find them, to carry them outside, and to see them shining in the light of the sun.

My mother was dead. For reasons that remained obscure, she'd decided to drive her car into a wall; before executing her plan, however, she'd written me a few lines, signing herself 'Mamma' for the first time. Accepting her role and dying had been, for her, the same thing.

My father was pootling around the deserted shopping centres of Busto Arsizio in his clapped-out car, with no comfort other than his thoughts, ever more alone, ever more desperate, enclosed in his intelligence as in a Plexiglas cage.

Not enough time had passed since your death; my childhood image of you was often overlaid by the memory of your face distorted with anger at those intrusive UFOs.

In that deserted house – where the only sound was the echo of my own footsteps – I was having more and more trouble breathing.

One night, I woke suddenly, feeling as if someone were crushing my throat. I gasped for air like a diver who's been submerged too long. From that day on, it became harder and harder for me to breathe. In my waking hours, I could feel my lungs contracting and popping like a pair of dry sponges; it wouldn't have taken very much pressure to crumble them to bits.

The dog days of summer were approaching. I sought the explanation for my growing malaise in psychology: I'm having difficulty breathing because I've cut the umbilical cord, I told myself.

In September, however, when I realised that I was inhabiting my clothes instead of wearing them, I decided to go to the doctor. And the doctor's visit led straight to the hospital. A virus had moved into my alveoli, where it was reproducing happily. I had a strain of pneumonia that produced no fever and no coughing but was nevertheless quite capable of causing death.

My hospital stay wasn't unhappy; there was always someone there to look after me and distract me without ever making me leave the bed. I made friends with a couple of ladies who shared my room. They were amazed that no one ever came to visit me.

The day I left, we exchanged addresses and false promises to see one another again. It was the second week of October. I walked the streets as though in a dream. The violent rush of sound and motion stunned me. I stepped along delicately, hesitantly.

Out in the garden, our rose bush was still in bloom – small, dense flowers, already preparing to face the cold – but the grass was beginning to turn yellow. In Buck's bowl, which was filled with rainwater, floated the corpses of a few wasps and one hornet. One month's absence had been enough to allow a stale, damp odour to pervade the house.

Autumn lay ahead of me, and around me, the void. I could sense the bora gathering itself beyond the Carpathians, and I could already feel it bearing down, surrounding me with its whistling, penetrating all the way inside my skull.

I couldn't face spending another winter here. It seemed to me as though I'd lived twenty years in the space of a few months, and I was too tired to go on.

I could certainly have come up with something to do – find a job, enrol at the university, experiment with love – but I would have done everything with only one hand, only one eye, only half a heart.

The truth, I knew, was that these wouldn't have been life choices so much as escapes, dodges, lids barely covering a seething pot. One part of me would have remained, reciting my make-believe part, while the other would have continued to wander about the world, moving with a Golem's hollow footsteps down every road, diving into every abyss, every darkness, waiting with trusting humility before every closed door, like a dog waiting for its as yet unknown master.

I wanted light. I wanted splendour.

I wanted either to discover whether or not truth exists

– whether or not everything turns on it, as in a kalei-
doscope – or to die.

The morning I went downtown to buy my ticket, I
witnessed a strange phenomenon. Although the sea was
calm, hundreds and hundreds of sole were moving up
the Canal Grande, swimming on the surface of the water
like flying carpets. When they reached the end of the
canal at the church of Sant'Antonio, they piled up in a
huge mass, unable to go any farther.

A small crowd of people gathered on the bridge,
curious and astonished as they watched this strange form
of mass suicide. There was much speculation. What was
going on? Was it a sign from heaven? Had a nuclear
submarine exploded? Was some foreign military power
testing a new kind of toxic weapon?

A few fishermen started lifting bucketfuls of sole out
of the water and dumping them into their boats. 'Are
they safe to eat?' the people on the bridge whispered.
'What do we know about what's really going on in the
world?'

Before their eyes, the fish were writhing and dying
one after another, in a welter of squirming bellies and
tails, while loudly shrieking seagulls darted through the
air above them. They came zooming in from all directions, white shapes plunging headlong from rooftops or
arriving from the sea in square formations like squads
of bombers. The surface of the water vibrated with the

energy of death; as soon as a gull ascended with its prey in its beak, the others flung themselves upon it, pursuing it implacably through the air and trying to snatch its prize.

The scene, at first once merely curious, had turned disturbing. Mothers and children stopped lingering on the bridge, and the groups of pensioners broke up.

Meanwhile, the normal, everyday life of the city continued. On the coast road, the usual line of vehicles waited for the green light. In the harbour, a cruise ship towed by a tugboat carried out its routine docking manoeuvres. In Ponterosso, deafening music (coming from a clothing store that catered to a young crowd) accompanied the lazy rituals of a few scattered market stalls.

Heaven's sending signs, but no one knows how to read them, I thought as I entered the shipping company's offices, which happened to face the Canal.

The next departure would be in exactly one week. The company official I spoke to told me that booking a cabin wouldn't be a problem – availability was good. In the modern world, who's crazy enough to waste five days travelling to a place you can reach in two hours by plane?

I reserved one of the cheapest interior cabins deep in the bowels of the ship.

As I returned home, I noticed I was walking with a lighter step. My decision to leave made me look upon things with detachment, almost with nostalgia. I hadn't tended the garden in months. The flower beds were filled with weeds, and bushes were growing promiscuously into one another. The hydrangeas and other flowers, dried up and browned by the season, seemed like a gathering of old schoolteachers wearing their mortar boards, while a blanket of leaves covered the garden almost entirely.

Leaves – they were one of your obsessions. Leaves and weeds. We had so many quarrels about leaves and/or weeds! You thought they were nuisances and as such had to be eliminated; I, on the other hand, was convinced that both were necessary. At some point, you'd accuse me of being lazy, and I'd counter by accusing you of knowing nothing about how to treat plants and trees. 'If leaves fall, there must be a reason,' I told you. 'Because nature's not nearly as stupid as man. And the plants you call weeds don't know they're weeds. You may judge them and condemn them, but they think they're flowers and herbs, as beautiful and important as all the rest.'

One day I shouted at you in exasperation. 'You don't see the soul of the garden!' I said. 'You don't see the soul of anything at all!'

I started calmly preparing for my departure. First I went to the bank to exchange some currency, and then I did some laundry and put moth repellent in the wardrobes. To avoid a grub invasion, I stored the rice, flour, and pasta in airtight containers. For a similar reason, I moved all the furniture out of the kitchen, for fear that some bits of food caught in the cracks would lead platoons of black caterpillars to colonise the floor and the ceiling.

During the next few days, I rather meticulously packed a knapsack with clothes and other necessities for my trip. Before closing the pack, I took the old coverless Bible I'd found in the attic and put it on top of everything else.

My father hadn't contacted me again. The bathing season was over, and he must have gone back to Grado Pineta. I didn't feel like calling him, so I wrote him a note.

'Dear Papa' didn't seem right, and so I threw away my first attempt. On the second sheet of paper, I wrote simply, 'I'm going on a trip to the land of your ancestors and mine.' Below those few words, I added the address of the place where, in all probability, I'd be staying.

The ship sailed in the early evening, after having swallowed up an interminable line of Albanian and Greek lorries. There was no restaurant on board, only a snack bar with plastic fittings and a neon light that gave every face a waxen, deathlike look.

Apart from the truck drivers, my fellow travellers included two busloads of retired Israelis returning from a trip to Europe. I watched them coming up from the belly of the ship, carrying boxes containing their cooking pots and eating utensils.

I went up on deck to look at the city as it disappeared into the distance.

The tugboat drew up alongside in order to take on the pilot. The beam from the lighthouse bounced off the surface of the sea at regular intervals. The black, calm water seemed to be a vast, threatening expanse of ink.

The stars shone above us, the same stars which, twenty years earlier, had shone above my mother and the little life that was growing in her womb. The noise of the powerful engines sounded almost reassuring during the few moments when I managed not to think about what was beneath.

Maybe the stars have eyes and see things as we see them, I thought. Maybe they have mysterious hearts and – as people have always believed – the ability to influence our actions. Maybe, on their white-hot edges, the dead live on, those who are no longer alive on earth, those who have already left behind one of the body's forms.

When I was very young, before I went to bed, I used to insist on looking out the window and waving to

Mamma, who, according to what you'd told me, had gone to live in heaven. On some evenings, if clouds covered the sky, I'd burst into tears. I imagined her as a fairy dressed in a long, light robe of coloured chiffon, wearing a dazzling cone covered with little stars on her head, a serene, slightly amused face, and, where her legs should have been, a single, luminous wake, which trailed out behind her as she followed me, fluttering from star to star.

But in fact, there was probably almost nothing left of her in her zinc coffin; and you, you were also decomposing down there, as I too would decompose one day.

What did our lives mean, then? What was the point of my mother's dreams for me and yours for her? Were we doomed to follow our destinies into the dark, or was there some meaning beyond the great emptiness?

Why did all of you – you, your mother, my father – abandon your roots? Out of fear, out of laziness, out of convenience? Or perhaps to be modern and free?

When I asked my father that question, he replied that Judaism was really nothing but an accretion of anthropological customs and social glue, and to prove his assertion, he offered the example of his own father, an extremely devout man as long as he was working for his father-in-law in Venice and frequenting his house, but ready to dance the samba without any regrets after burying his wife in Brazil.

And you once told me we had no religion. We weren't anything at all. When you saw that this worried me, you added, 'It's not a bad way to be, you know. In fact, it's good. It means you're free, and freedom is the only true wealth a person can have.'

Is this the reason why my soul's like a dog's soul? Is this the reason why I've always roamed the streets so anxiously, plagued with the ferocious restlessness of those who have no master?

Roots

12

After six days of tranquil navigation, we arrived in the port of Haifa.

Standing on deck, watching the city grow larger, I had the impression that it was strangely familiar, that it reminded me of Trieste. Behind it, instead of the Kras, but equally rocky, rose the spurs of Mount Carmel; multi-storey buildings jutted up everywhere – the newest ones were also the most horrible. On the left, where the hilly ground yielded to the plain, dense smoke from a series of industrial plants rose into the air and mingled with the flames of a refinery.

But Haifa doesn't have a seafront like Trieste's. Instead of the coast road and the Piazza d'Unità, there were mooring docks for cargo ships, and over them towered a range of yellow cranes with their long arms hanging down. At their feet, dozens of container ships from all over the world were piled up, one on top of another.

Although the counter-terrorism officers had already come on board at Limassol in Cyprus, the disembarcation took forever. While waiting for clearance to go ashore, I loitered on the deck for a while, staring at the outline of a strange building that stood atop the hill, framed by terraced gardens sloping down toward the sea; the building's round, golden cupola suggested a mosque, but without a minaret next to it.

'What's that?' I asked a lady from Ashkelon whom I'd met during the voyage.

'That? It's the Bahá'í temple,' she said, smiling as if to add, *Just what we need*. In fact, it housed the tomb of Bahá'u'lláh, a Persian who broke away from Islam in the latter half of the nineteenth century and founded his own syncretic religious movement, based on universal love among men of all faiths and races.

As I stepped on to dry land, I became aware of the great weight of the knapsack on my back, as heavy as the century that was drawing to a close, and I knew that the time had come for me to stop and examine the contents of my burden, to take out all the stones, one by one, and finally give them names, to catalogue them, and then to decide which I should continue to carry and which I should leave behind.

All at once, on that unknown yet somehow familiar soil, I understood that our personal story is also the story of those who preceded us and of the choices they made. Those choices have formed us; like calcium carbonate inside a cave, they're the invisible structure of each individual.

Rather than a blank slate on which anything at all can be written, a newborn baby is a tablecloth into which someone has already woven a pattern. Will the child follow the path already marked out by others, or will he choose a different one? Will he keep treading the familiar furrow, or will he have the nerve to spring out of it with both feet? And why does one person tear out the pattern while another blindly, diligently follows the design?

And then, is this life really the only one we have? Is this the sole lighted space given us to cross? Is it not perhaps too awful and cruel to gamble everything in a single existence? To understand, to not understand, to mistake, to collide? One heartbeat separates birth from death; we open our mouths to say, 'Oh!' in horror, then 'Oh!' in wonder, and then everything's over? Must we resign ourselves to keeping quiet and stretching out our necks like the latest in a long line of sacrificial victims? To coming into the world and then sinking into death like a house of cards that silently falls in on itself?

And who decides the roles before the performance? Which one will be assigned to me: the victim, or the executioner? Or is everything just an endless succession of light and shade?

To kill or to be killed: Who decides that? Maybe those who find themselves in the pool of light. But the ones in the shadows, what do they do? And how about me? Where am I supposed to stand? Is it true that everything takes place as though on a stage – entrances, exits, blown or forgotten lines? And what happens to the victims' death rattles and the cold sweats of their final agonies and their wretched nights, inhabited only by their physiology? Is there some place in heaven that contains all that, a catalogue, an archive, a cosmic memory? And, along with the mere record, a scale, and maybe someone who weighs existences? How do the right- and left-hand weighing pans balance each other: actions on one side, with judgement as the counterweight on the other? Does Michael's sword flame out, darting here and there, or is it the whirr of nothingness that reverberates through space?

Or is the universe perhaps just a vast rumen, filled with black holes that grind up and absorb all forms of energy? Is the meaning of the world to be found in this indefatigable motor, in this mastication-absorption-excretion engine, in this symphony of gastric juices?

But when the rumen closes, the cow dies.

And what about the universe?

Are we proteins, minerals, amino acids, fluids, enzymatic reactions, and nothing else? Whitish larvae, wiggling about, devouring, and being devoured? But even the larva can know the dignity of transformation; its soft tissue can produce the unexpected splendour of a butterfly.

And what if the magic word were indeed 'transformation'? If the darkness existed precisely in order to welcome the Light?

13

Of all the family stories, the one about Uncle Ottavio was the most famous.

You gave me only a hint of it one evening when we were sitting on the sofa and looking at some family photographs you'd taken out of a chest. How old was I? Ten or twelve – I'd already reached the stage where the absence of a face (my father's) had started to torment me. You couldn't show me his picture, as you didn't know who he was, and maybe you were trying somehow to fill the empty space that was spreading inside me.

I remember a succession of anonymous images, harking back to a period that seemed to me to have taken place shortly after the disappearance of the dinosaurs.

The most frequently photographed location was the big white villa, surrounded by a park, where you grew up. It was the setting for a family reunion, servants included, posing before a cricket match, and for many other snapshots, including several of your dog Argo, he of the intelligent eyes, stretched out in front of the entrance to the greenhouse. There were images of the villa in its summer splendour, with rose-covered arbours scattered around the lawn and shutters open on flowery balconies, and then there was a shot of the villa after the bombers destroyed it: a pile of debris under a cloud of black smoke.

Many of the photos showed you as a child with a big ribbon in your hair, or with your parents in a photographer's studio, posed before a bombastically painted backdrop; then there was a picture of your mother alone, posing as she sang. There were photographs of various other children – all of them in the obligatory sailor's costume, holding hoops or miniature violins and wearing little boots buttoned up above the ankle – whose names and degree of kinship you declaimed to me with the best of intentions but without arousing the slightest interest. What did I care about all those characters, who to my eyes looked as though they'd stepped out of a period film, or about that luxurious villa, which had gone up in smoke the day Mike from Alabama or someone like him, piloting his fighter-bomber, decided to press the button and release the bombs?

Once, while we were driving past the place where the villa used to be, you showed me a solitary cedar,

surrounded by dozens of dismal blocks of flats black-
ened by smoke from the ironworks. 'You see that tree?'
you said. 'My seesaw was balanced on its lowest
branches.'

That soot-covered conifer was the only survivor from
the large park that had surrounded your family's villa.

Uncle Ottavio was your mother's brother; you showed
me a photograph of him, sitting at a piano while his
sister stood beside him, singing a romantic song. In a
family where more or less everyone played a musical
instrument for pleasure, he was the only one who made
music his profession. A much-admired pianist, he gave
concerts throughout Europe. He toured continually, and
when he was home, he spent most of his time practising
in the living room.

You couldn't stand him, you told me, but you added
that perhaps you were only jealous of his talent, seeing
that you had no talents at all. He married – rather late
for those days – a harpist from Gorizia, and they had
two children, a girl and a boy, several years apart. The
girl, Allegra, inherited her parents' musical aptitude, and
after graduating from the conservatoire in Trieste, she
moved to America to perfect her viola studies. Her
younger brother, Gionata, moved to Israel at the end of
the Second World War.

'Why Israel?' I asked, with my customary anxiety. 'Had he fallen in love?'

You stiffened at that question. 'In love?' you repeated. Then, with a faraway look in your eyes, you added, 'Yes, maybe so . . . in a way . . . but it's a long story, and it's also a little sad: too long and too sad for a little girl who has to go to bed.'

My protests availed me nothing. I loved sad fairy-tales; every evening I fell asleep hugging the Little Mermaid, repeating the most desperate tales underneath the sheets while the Ugly Duckling watched me from the bedside table.

'But this isn't a fairytale,' you said, cutting me off, and that was all there was to it. And so my great-great uncle, his wife, his piano, the harp, the viola, Allegra, Gionata, and his (to me) strange destination all disappeared into the pitch-black well of non-time.

I brought three letters I'd found in the attic on the trip with me. Two of them came from the United States; the first was from Allegra, and the second was signed by Sara, one of her daughters, who wrote to announce her mother's death. The third letter had arrived from Israel: In a few unadorned lines, your cousin Gionata congratulated you on Ilaria's birth and announced that he'd got married and settled permanently on a piece of land north of the Sea of Galilee. The letter contained his complete address, just in case you might want to visit him someday.

That address was my destination after I disembarked in Haifa. Given that Gionata was the son of the youngest of your mother's brothers, I figured he would be in his seventies and most probably still alive. In this part of the hemisphere – which left out the bunch of mulatto cousins I probably had on the beaches of Rio de Janeiro – your cousin Gionata was my only surviving relative, apart from my father. I thought of him as more of an uncle than a cousin.

The bus that would carry me to my destination didn't stop very far from where I was. I waited for less than an hour, and then I was able to climb aboard. Air conditioning and music were both going full blast, and most of the seats were taken by young men and women in military uniforms. With great nonchalance, some of them carried submachine guns slung over their shoulders.

The bus left Haifa from the north, the side opposite Mount Carmel, and crossed the industrial zone, which was dominated by great viaducts. I looked through my window, watching warehouses, workshops, supermarkets and car dealerships file past. The traffic was fairly chaotic, and the drivers gesticulated threateningly through their open windows, blowing their horns again and again. Strangely, I felt not agitated but rather suspended; soon I'd reach the kibbutz indicated in the letter. I had no idea whether I'd really be able to find my uncle; maybe he'd been dead for a long time or maybe he'd changed his address. Maybe I'd find some cousin who'd stayed behind, or maybe – the worst possibility – I'd find nobody at all.

Not even that hypothesis sufficed to worry me, because I was certain of one thing: my trip wasn't an escape (as my trip to the States had been). This time, I was moving *towards* something; I was going to confront something I had no knowledge of but which nevertheless concerned me deeply.

I stepped out of the bus – the only passenger who did – and on to the shoulder of a road that ran through fields. In front of me, a gate reinforced with barbed wire protected a construction that was a cross between a sentry box and a porter's lodge.

I walked up to the armed guard, a young man, and told him my name and the name of the person I was looking for. The guard and I stepped into the field together. While I was on the bus, I'd tried to imagine what a kibbutz would look like; my mental image, based on stories one of your friends had told me, featured an arrangement of spartan shacks huddled together on a plot of parched land.

But as I followed the young soldier, I thought that the kibbutz I was entering looked less like a pioneer village and more like a university campus. Small, one-storey houses, each of them graced with a lawn and a small garden, were scattered here and there. The communal amenities even included a swimming pool and a tennis court. In the centre of the field rose a building taller and more spacious than the others; this, my guide informed me, was the dining room.

The only real differences between this place and a campus were the pervasive smell of manure and the presence, in the distance, of several large silos.

Bougainvillea with bracts of every colour, from fuchsia and magenta to yellow and white, adorned practically every wall. The vines spread out exuberantly, almost arrogantly. Large numbers of sparrows flitted among the flowers and leaves.

My young companion indicated that I should wait. I slipped off my backpack and sat down on a bench, looking around uncertainly. I wasn't completely sure he'd understood who it was I was looking for; maybe I didn't explain myself very well, I thought. However, after waiting for about fifteen minutes, I saw a white-bearded man of average height detach himself from a small group of people, and I recognised him (thanks to the mysterious laws of genetics) at once and unequivocally as Uncle Gionata.

My uncle was visibly taken by surprise, but he didn't seem particularly disturbed by my presence. Although his original given name was Gionata, he hadn't spoken Italian for many years. As far as he was concerned, his name was now Jonathan, but he addressed me in the same rather old-fashioned idiom that you would use every now and then when you were ill.

He insisted that we should go to his house – a squat, prefabricated dwelling facing a small, blooming garden – to have a cup of tea. Despite his age, my uncle maintained a strong, lean physique. His manner of speaking was very direct.

I told him about you – I said you had died about a year ago – about my mother, who'd passed away when I was four years old (I omitted any allusion to the voluntary nature of her death), and finally about my father, a philosophy professor who lived in Grado and who had nothing to do with me when I was growing up.

Uncle Jonathan had recently lost his wife, who'd passed away a couple of months after being diagnosed with what's become the most common of diseases. Two children had been born of their marriage: the older, Arik, was an engineer living in Arad; his younger sister worked as a psychiatrist in the hospital at Beersheba.

Uncle Jonathan was the proud grandfather of twin girls, Arik's daughters, now seven years old; both of them had begun playing the violin at a very tender age, and thanks to the method invented by the Japanese violinist Shin'ichi Suzuki, they'd already been able to show that they'd inherited in the highest degree the musical talent of two of their great-grandparents, Uncle Ottavio and his harpist wife. Jonathan had recently returned from Arad, where he'd attended, with great emotion, a performance by the two little girls.

Strangely enough, he told me, the music that had nourished his childhood had suddenly disappeared when he left Italy; he'd stopped listening to records and going to concerts. The only music that accompanied his daily life in Israel was the sound of tractors. In fact, from the day he'd moved there, the land had been his sole occupation. It was he who'd planted the long rows of grapefruit trees that extended all the way to the slopes of the hills, and he was also responsible for the avocado orchards.

Before Jonathan and his fellow kibbutzniks arrived, there had been nothing here but rocks and weeds. They'd spent the first years loosening and spading the soil by hand, and then they'd brought in the tractors. Since Jonathan had always been passionate about mechanical things, he'd taken a course in tractor repair. The kibbutzniks wanted to be self-sufficient in everything; this was the philosophy that had inspired them to build their community bit by bit, year by year.

The younger generation no longer cared anything

about these ancient choices made by their forebears. They wanted everything, right away. They didn't know how to wait; they weren't capable of self-sacrifice for the future of the community – or perhaps they didn't have enough strength of character. 'That's why I'm bitter,' Uncle Jonathan confided to me. 'And so are the other people of my age. Whose fault was it? Was it our fault, or was it just the times? I shouldn't take it so hard. Ever since the world began, the young have tended to destroy everything their parents built, and life goes on all the same . . . Ah well, maybe these are just the sad grumblings of an old man.'

He put me up in what he called the 'guest room': a narrow space with plywood walls, where there was barely enough room for a chair and a camp bed. A single window framed the aromatic branches of a eucalyptus tree.

I'd never heard hoopoes and turtle-doves sing so ebulliently. It was as if the sun, which beat down on that land with greater intensity, had infused everything with greater vigour. The flowers were bigger and more colourful; the birds sang at a more stirring pitch. Did the same hold true for feelings, perhaps – for love and for hate, for the violent power of memory?

I fell asleep pondering that question.

When I heard knocking at my door, I thought it was still the middle of the night. It was my uncle, wanting to have breakfast with me. As it turned out, it was almost five o'clock, and the sun was already high in the sky. When Uncle Jonathan saw my dismayed face, he excused himself, explaining that he had to be in the fields as early as possible, before it became too hot to work.

The big dining room was already filled with people. Their voices mingled and echoed like the chatter of guests at a wedding banquet.

That first morning, I wandered around the kibbutz and didn't see Uncle Jonathan again until lunchtime. 'Look at all those blond heads and blue eyes,' he said, assuming an air of satisfaction as we passed near the nursery schoolyard, which was full of children at play. 'Hitler would have had a stroke.'

At home, the old, noisy air conditioner was already on. I sat on the narrow sofa in the living room and noticed an old print, a view of Trieste, hanging on the wall across from me. The picture showed a section of the seashore with the Palazzo Carciotti in the background: ladies with umbrellas, gentlemen with walking sticks and top hats, and nurses with baby carriages promenaded along the San Carlo pier (today known as the Audace), while crates of every size were being unloaded from a long line of ships in the Canal Grande.

I walked over to the print and studied it more closely. 'What were they unloading?' I asked my uncle.

'Well . . . coffee, for the most part, but also spices and

fabrics. You know why I keep that on the wall? Because it makes me think of a time that doesn't exist any more, a time when you could spend hours and hours passionately discussing a whole range of topics ... a performance of Bizet's *Carmen*, for example – whether or not it was better than the one you'd heard last year – or nearly come to blows defending your favourite poet. My wife didn't like that print. She maintained that the past was past and that we shouldn't allow it to keep sticking to us, but that picture gave me a kind of ... I won't say peace, but at least relief. It was a comfort to me to know that once upon a time, there had been an era – my father's era – when you could talk about art as though it were the most important thing in the world; a period when horror was still confined to the background. Not that horror didn't exist – there's always been horror in the heart of man – but no one talked about it, it couldn't be seen, and you could still live as though it didn't exist; it remained compressed within the official spaces of war.

'You see,' he went on, 'my parents were convinced – maybe because they were artists, or maybe because the times were different – that beauty was the light that illuminated the human heart. My father used to tell me, "Music can open any door"; my mother would bring me out into the garden to listen to the ways different leaves rustled.

'They were idealists, certainly. Had they lived a bit

more in the real world, maybe they could have avoided at least part of the tragedy, but that was the way they were – they always looked on the bright side of things. They were convinced that beauty and moral probity must go hand in hand. The memories of the years I spent with them in the villa are suffused with a kind of golden light. There were no shadows between them, and nothing clouded their relationship with us. For their time, I think they were pretty unconventional. They played with us children, but our education always came first. The principles they required us to adopt were few, but they had to be respected with the utmost strictness. At the dinner table, any subject was fair game for discussion; no question was dodged.

'I remember once – I must have been six or seven, the age when you begin to wonder about things – I asked a question, point-blank, at lunch. I said, "So who made the world?"

'"God created the world," my father replied.

'"And after he created it," my mother added, "he created music, too, so that people could understand it."

'Unlike most marriages in those days – and, come to think of it, nowadays – their union wasn't limited to a physical attraction or an infatuation due to factors that could change. They truly loved each other. I never knew them to speak harshly to each other or to be in a huff. Sometimes they had very lively discussions, but they never showed any of the malevolence that comes to the surface when one is tired of life or one feels disappointed.

'I think a major contributing factor in all of this was the relationship they had with harmony, with music. Once they entered the domain of beauty, they were able to dissolve any conflict.

'Their naivety was in believing that what had value for them could be valuable to others, that all human beings had in common an interior tension capable of giving things light.

'I don't know how often I've brooded over this through the years, how many times I've deconstructed and reconstructed every hour, every minute, every second of our life together. It was as though I was working on a tractor engine but couldn't figure out what was wrong with it.

'You could almost say I lived only half a life. My wife was always asking me, "Where are you? Are you with us, or are you travelling in the time machine?"

'No, I don't think I was a good husband or even a good father. I was always only half what I should have been.

'Besides, I often tell myself, when a life is broken apart it can't be put back together again. All you can do is fake it, you can put some glue on the fragments, but your repair job will always show. "Broken" means you've got two or three or four parts inside you that can't ever be properly repaired. And it means that if you want to go on living, you have to try to put the pieces together so they'll at least function without audible squeals and squeaks.

'My parents, constantly wrapped up in the harmony of their music, slipped into the awful conviction that the human heart was fundamentally good, and that the worst, most hardened criminal possessed this goodness, precisely because it was innate. All that was necessary was to awaken the natural goodness inside him – with a smile, with a song, with a flower.

'They weren't religious, at least not in the traditional sense. My father's father had converted to Christianity. I don't think he was struck down on the road to Damascus – he had his vision on the road to practicality. His family had been agnostics for some time, so crossing over from one side to the other wasn't a very earth-shaking move.

'My mother's family, however, still belonged in name – though not in fact – to the tradition. They went to the synagogue, but only for weddings and circumcisions.

'I think my mother considered the various customs and practices that had been imposed upon her as a kind of folklore, but she wasn't an atheist at all, or even an agnostic. She believed in a supreme being, loved to read books on spiritual subjects, and was deeply interested in the transmigration of souls – reincarnation, in other words. She followed the ideas of a Russian noblewoman named Blavatsky or something like that.

'I remember once looking at a hairy caterpillar on a leaf in the garden and saying, "Tomorrow you'll be a butterfly, but who were you before?"

'I found it very troubling to think that there could be a reality hidden behind things, which were not, in short, what they appeared to be. I wasn't a worthy son. I never had much imagination or grand fantasies, and in the end I dedicated myself to motors and not to metaphysics. One day I caught myself thinking, it's better that they're dead, because they might have been ashamed of such an ordinary son, and then I was ashamed of having had that thought.

'Now that I'm alone in the house – it was different when my wife and children were here – and I know I don't have a lot of time left, I often stay up very late. I listen to the traffic noise as it diminishes, hour by hour, and I hear the jackals. What can their howls be, if not questions addressed to the moon, to the stars, to the sky?

'As I peer out towards the yelping jackals, I can see the vapours rising from the earth. My mother is in that dense, dark cloud, her essence mixed with thousands of others – her dreams, her talent, her gaze, all ashes scattered on the Vistula, on the trees, on the fields around Birkenau. The potassium from those bodies has made entire regions fertile and helped bring to life tall snow-drops, enormous savoy cabbages, apples big as globes.

'But is my mother really buried in all that, in that triumph of biochemistry, or is that just her hair and her bones? Has her soul really moved into a new body, as she believed, the way you change from one hotel room to another when you're on a trip? Maybe she's been reincarnated in Africa or in some remote village in the Andes . . .

'At night, my thoughts become immense, but in that immensity I never think of Paradise, a place where one can live without guilt, suspended in a lightness with nothing human about it. That would mean someone's watching over us, and I don't believe that, not at all. There's no one who cares about the destiny of the human race, much less about individual humans.

'In my life, I've tried to conduct myself in the best possible way, to be honest, to work, to raise a family and love it according to my capacity, and that's all; that's the only thing I have to set upon the scale. A limited offering, no doubt, but as is the case with every limita-tion, I'm not the one who set it.

'I came here after the war to escape my memories. No pleasant tie bound me to Europe any more, and I wanted to understand who I was, to rebuild a kind of identity for myself, and I slowly succeeded in doing so.

'I have no regrets. I wouldn't go back for anything

in the world, but it's not like I was struck down by some vision. I'm a sceptic, as I always was. A sceptic with good will, but still a sceptic.

'You see that?' my uncle continued, pointing at a sort of rectangular box attached to the door. 'My son put that there. It's a mezuzah. Arik has always been a very religious boy, even though we never encouraged him in that direction. At home, we confined ourselves to strictly respecting the traditions, but that's all. Naturally, we didn't discourage him either, but every now and then his mother and I, together or separately, would look at him as though he were a stranger and wonder, "Where did he come from?"

'We couldn't arrive at an answer.

'Sometimes I found myself thinking that his grand-mother's soul really must have transmigrated into his body. I thought Arik's deep piety could only be a way for my mother to expiate her passion for Madame Blavatsky and for all the rest of her cockeyed spiritual-istic readings.

'My wife used to say that being born is like getting dropped off the top of a very high building. Therefore, falling is our destiny, and so we must try to hold on to something. One person may cling to a window sill, another to a balcony, another will clutch a shutter, and yet another will manage, at the last possible moment, to grab the edge of the gutter. If you want to live, you have to look for something to hold on to, and it doesn't much matter what that something is. But my wife saw things differently. She came from an observant family, and she'd never got on with her father, who was a rather rigid man. At bottom, you always want what isn't in the house, and maybe that was one of the reasons why my wife couldn't hide her irritation at that son of ours, who was trying to push the traditional ways she'd managed to kick out back in through the window.

'I, on the other hand, have always been convinced that Arik's beliefs are truly and deeply held. I remember an episode that goes back to when he was thirteen or fourteen. It was the Sabbath, and at some point he came into the house and found his mother on the telephone with her sister in Tel Aviv. He burst into desperate tears and shouted, "Why can't you live a holy life?"

'You see? Human affairs are always extraordinarily complex. That's why I say that the most important issue is honesty. If you start from there, you can go anywhere.'

Although it was barely six o'clock, night had already fallen, and a light breeze, blowing seaward from the hills, had arisen with the darkness. Outside the window, the bougainvillea moved with a rustle like tissue paper; from the nearby cowsheds came the mooing of a young calf, a desperate appeal to which there was no response. Maybe its mother had already been taken to the slaughterhouse. Uncle Jonathan poured himself a glass of water and drank it down in one breath. The air conditioner was off, and it was very hot. It must have been a long time since my uncle had talked so much; with a sigh, he let himself fall against the back of the sofa and looked at me hard. 'How about you?' he asked. 'What do you believe in?'

14

The weight of night is the weight of unanswerable questions. Night is the time of the sick and the anxious; there's no escaping its tyranny. You can turn on a light, open a book, search the radio for a comforting voice, but the night still remains, lying in wait for you. We come out of darkness and return to darkness; before the universe was formed, all space was darkness.

Maybe that's the reason why cities are always bright and filled with distractions: at any hour of the night, if you wish, you can go out to eat, buy something, have a good time. Silence and darkness are relegated to those few hours when you're about to keel over from exhaustion and need to recuperate a bit before you can go on, but what you fall into isn't a restless slumber shot through with nagging questions; it's a faint – that's the proper word for it – a brief period of time during which the body is compelled to yield to physiology. And then you wake up in front of a bright screen, and the only person who can operate the remote control is you.

My uncle had asked me what I believed in. Surrounded by the nocturnal silence, I twisted and turned in my bed and found no rest. I knew sleep wouldn't come, but I hoped (in vain) I might at least grow somewhat drowsy. Uncle Jonathan's question revolved in the air around me, towing in its wake many other questions, chief among them its twin: Why do you live?

What do you believe in? Why do you live? At birth, every child should receive a parchment sheet with those two questions written on it, awaiting answers. Later, when all the actions of his life have been performed, the former child will have that same sheet with him when he presents himself for death.

In fact, if we could cancel out night and silence, then there would be no place left for questions – and so the purpose of the parchment sheet would be to ensure that no child believes himself an object, even the most perfect of objects, and that every former child knows (should he chance to spend a sleepless night in later years) that he's not being kept awake by a sickness, but by his nature; because man alone, and no other creature, has the ability to ask himself questions.

What do you believe in?

You can believe in so many things, including the first

thing you come across. For example, when a child eats his pap, he's convinced it's the best in the world, never having tasted any other; if an egg hatches in front of a cat, the newborn chick thinks the feline is its parent and solicits it for food.

You can consent to eat the same pap all your life, or at a certain point you can refuse it, turning your face aside like a child who's had enough.

Or maybe you can realise that no one's handing out any food, and after that realisation you're hungry and thirsty and afflicted with non-stop nervousness. When you've reached this point, the only way to calm down is to move, to take a walk, to wander around asking others – and yourself – questions, looking for a knowing face, for someone who can answer them.

So what do you believe in?

I believe in pain, which is the master of my life. Pain is what possesses me from the moment I open my eyes, pervades my body and my mind, electrifies, devastates, deforms; it's what has made me unfit to live; it's what has put a ticking time bomb in my heart and set the fuse for a probable explosion.

My first memories are filled with pain instead of joy, with anxiety and fear instead of the tranquil security of belonging. While I prowled around our flat, searching for my mother among people who had passed out from various excesses, while I watched her sleeping beside a companion who was never the same as the last one, how could I feel anything but lost? Even then, I knew instinctively that I was a child begotten not by love but by accident, and this perception, instead of making me bitter or resentful, stirred in me a strange desire to protect my mother. I always detected a hint of sadness under her forced cheer; I felt she was adrift, heading for disaster, and I would have given my life to avoid it.

Where does my soul come from? Was it formed when I was, or does it spring from the mystery of time beyond time? Did it perhaps descend to earth, contravening the laws of nature, in order to help a body that had summoned it inadvertently and thus condemned it to a life of suffering and alienation, to the uneasiness of belonging nowhere, of thinking that, as my father once said, 'It doesn't matter from what or for whom I'm here, since everything, from mould to elephants, reproduces itself inexorably'?

Was I, therefore, a daughter of inexorability?

Often, on the nights when the bora is blowing in Trieste, a small crowd of demonstrators gathers in front of the Palazzo di Giustizia, the court, to protest some abuse of power, and inveighs against it with ever-increasing anger until dawn.

Is it fate that's locked up inside the Palazzo di Giustizia, protected by bars and guards? Is it hiding there because it's afraid? Must we address our questions to fate? And what should it hide from, if not human questioning? What should shame it, if not the inexorability it's flung upon the stage of the world, without so much as a hint of explanation?

Fate stayed on my mind, so I decided to get up. It was still dark; the clock radio flashed 3 a.m. In a few houses, the lights were already on. At night, fate has to confront a great many supplicants; every lamp signals some disquiet, some fracture, an incomplete bridge. Every light's a restless memory, I thought, walking along the perimeter of a citrus orchard.

I reached the far end of the field and sat down on a rock. The night breeze had died down; everything, including noises and smells, was immobile. I felt as though I were in an auditorium before the beginning of a concert; the members of the orchestra were all in position, the conductor was poised on the podium, but his arm had yet to move. Eyes, minds, hearts, muscles – all were standing by, ready to burst into a harmony of sound.

It was still dark when a cock crowed in the Arab village up on the slopes of the hill. A short while later, a glimmer of light began to suffuse the dark vault of the sky.

As I went back into the field, I heard modulated singing coming from one of the cottages. Someone was praying in the solitude of the dawn. Was it a prayer of thanksgiving or a plea? I wondered about that on the way back to my bed. Didn't all nocturnal questions arise in the same way? Suppose questions were nothing but the only form of prayer that has been granted us?

The following week, I began working on the kibbutz, lending a hand wherever one was needed. It was a period when there was little activity in the fields, so for the most part I helped in the kitchen or the big laundry room.

One evening, Uncle Jonathan told me his father's story, the story you never wished to include among the stories you preferred, such as *The Little Mermaid* or *The Ugly Duckling*.

The atmosphere in Trieste had grown heavy with menace. Uncle Jonathan's parents had many friends who'd already emigrated to safety, not before advising the two of them to do the same. But Ottavio, Uncle Jonathan's father, didn't want to leave; he rebelled at the very thought of the word 'flee'. He said, 'Why should I run away? That's what thieves do, and murderers, wrongdoers, cowards, people with something to hide. But what wrong have I done?'

'That absolute tranquillity didn't come from knowing that he was a baptised Christian,' Uncle Jonathan explained. 'It was due to a genuine interior distance from what was happening around him. He couldn't grasp that it was possible for one man to kill another solely because of his surname.'

'I'm an Italian citizen!' Ottavio declared when they came to get him, as if his geographical affiliation entitled him to a magical safe-conduct pass.

Uncle Jonathan was out at the time of the arrests. As he was returning home, he realised what was going on and fell into step with a lady who was coming down from the Carso, as she'd done for years, to bring his family butter. Counting on his blond hair and blue eyes to save him, he'd pretended to be her son and watched in mute helplessness as his parents were brought out under arrest.

Uncle Jonathan told me he didn't return to the villa. The woman from the dairy took him back to her place on the plateau, and he stayed there until the end of the war. Lost in thought, he added, 'Maybe that was when I made my choice between the earth and books. I chose the earth. In printed language there were questions and nothing else, but in the fields there was life, and life went on. It simply went on.'

In the following weeks, the bishop, a longtime admirer of Ottavio's musical talent, had managed with the help of pressure from influential friends to win his freedom, but as the safe-conduct was valid for only one person, Ottavio had refused it.

On Yom Kippur in 1944, his parents had left Italy for the desolate plains of Poland, where his mother soon vanished without a trace. As for his father, three months after the end of the war, the Red Cross had informed Uncle Jonathan that his father Ottavio was still alive.

'In the autumn of 1945,' Uncle Jonathan continued, 'my father returned to Trieste, almost unrecognisable physically but apparently unchanged in spirit. He immediately summoned his former piano tuner; after the old fellow left, Ottavio sat down and began to play. It seemed that he needed nothing else. He wasn't interested in eating, drinking, sleeping, or taking a walk – all he wanted to do was play music, and that was enough for him. At first, I thought that music and its central role in his life had probably made a major contribution to his survival, but I was soon forced to change my mind on that score.'

One month after his return, Uncle Ottavio started announcing – insistently – his desire to perform in concert. His request was soon granted.

Jonathan's memory of the evening had remained vivid. The auditorium was packed and the audience attentive; not a fly buzzed, no one sneezed, no one coughed. Everyone seemed carried away by the almost metaphysical intensity of his father's performance. The pianist's very face seemed transfigured. As the audience watched him, an uneasy feeling came over everyone, including his son.

Who was this person playing? Was it his father, the man he'd always known, or did he merely resemble him? His hands ran up and down the keyboard, but there was no joy left in his eyes; a cold, distant light seemed to be drawing him far, far away, into a place where it was impossible to reach him.

When it was over, the audience rose to its feet and gave him an ovation ten minutes long, demanding an encore, but Uncle Ottavio returned to the stage, bowed gravely, and then froze the hall with a sharp, slashing, one-handed gesture from left to right, as if to say no, it's impossible. Don't insist. I've finished.

Many people murmured, 'Unforgettable, truly unforgettable,' as they retrieved their overcoats in the lobby. It wasn't clear whether they were referring to the concert or to its unusual close.

The following day, Uncle Ottavio got up, threw all his scores into the stove, closed the lid of his piano, slipped on his overcoat, and went out.

From that day forward – including all winter long – going out was his sole activity. He'd leave the house at dawn and return long after nightfall. Every now and then, someone who knew him reported that they'd seen him walking along the seashore in Muggia or Aurisina. He strode along with his head down and never recognised anybody. Friends greeted him and he marched straight on without acknowledging them. His lips moved constantly, as if he were having an animated discussion with himself. He stopped bathing, stopped shaving, and wore the same filthy overcoat and hopelessly ruined hiking boots and a cap pulled down over his eyes. He kept several lengths of rope wrapped around his waist.

After a few months, he began to use that rope to bring dogs home.

The first two were a couple of mutts of the hunting-dog variety; he made a place for them at the back of the yard, in the area near the garage. He stayed home for a week, building some rudimentary mesh kennels; once they were finished, he took up his wanderings again. He went out in the morning and came home in the evening, always leading a new dog tied to the end of one of his ropes.

'It didn't take long,' Uncle Jonathan recalled, 'before the situation became intolerable. The animals made messes everywhere, they barked and howled and mangled one another scrapping for food. Admittedly, my father didn't feed them regularly, only when he remembered to or felt like it, and no one else was allowed to give them food in his place. He caught me feeding them once and rushed at me like a madman. If the dogs fought, he'd throw himself into the fray, deal out blows left and right with his stick until the fighting stopped, and fall to the ground exhausted; however, if they'd eaten their fill and settled down, he'd spend hours stroking them, all the while speaking to them in a calm, soothing voice. He'd sit in their midst, talking to them as if they were children: "You've got loving hearts," he'd say, "loving hearts. Not like some . . ." And the dogs would wag their tails and brush his hand softly with their quick tongues.

'It was obvious that he needed to be hospitalised and treated, but how? He would never have agreed to enter a hospital, and I couldn't force him to.

'It was a very delicate matter. How could we help him? Was it still possible? And, above all, was it right? Did he really want to go back to being the pianist of old, or had that peremptory gesture at the end of his last concert marked a definitive watershed between before and after, between what he'd been and what he'd been forced to become? That dividing line, which marked the death of beauty – that line must also have signalled the beginning of his posthumous life.

'Probably, we shouldn't have tried to cure him but rather ourselves, our inability to tolerate devastation, to bear the sight of good being corrupted into evil. After all, in the beginning we'd all deluded ourselves into thinking we'd be able to go on as if nothing had happened. If there's a little evil, you can stand it, you can even observe it, but is that possible when evil's so dark and dense it covers the whole horizon?

'Fortunately, death, at least sometimes, is merciful. One day when I came home, I didn't hear the dogs barking, but I didn't give it much thought. It was only a little later, when I looked out the bathroom window and noticed how still they were, that I rushed out into the yard and found him.

'There he was, lying with his eyes open among the kennels. He seemed to be smiling. His heart had stopped suddenly and painlessly. Instead of biting him and tearing at him, the animals were watching over his body in silence, wagging their tails in turn, as if communicating with one another. They say that dogs are able to see the angel of death. At that moment, I believed the saying was true. I thought maybe the dogs themselves were angels, because of the way they offered their hearts to their master. In any case, I had the consolation of seeing that he had died calmly. A modest relief, which vanishes into thin air at night, when I reflect that, in all probability, even the most vicious criminals die with such an expression on their faces.'

15

After dinner that evening, when I was back in my room, I started reading the Bible. As my education hadn't prepared me for Bible study, my reading didn't proceed in any very orderly fashion. I confined myself to opening the volume at random, scanning the text, and then repeating the process, looking for a passage that would resonate. With all the reading that we did together, I wonder why you never suggested the Bible. Were you afraid of influencing me too much? Or did you fear you wouldn't be able to answer my questions firmly and truly?

And was that the reason why you never spoke to me about Uncle Ottavio?

You probably decided to put off any reference to that subject until I was old enough to understand it; later, when I'd finally reached the appropriate age, you were overwhelmed by how restless and unhappy I was, and soon all that violent emotion was followed by the devastation of your illness, and so the right time for evoking these memories never came.

What roots did you provide me with?

You gave me love, certainly, but what was its foundation, what nourished it, what pushed it beyond natural genetic impulses?

And why weren't you able to love my mother? What caused you to let her go adrift, like a rudderless boat?

Wasn't there anything you could have done?

Or does the flow of time, of history, always drag lives along, always carry them away? Was my mother just a daughter of her time, as you were of yours and I am of mine?

And suppose history is indeed a flowing current, I thought, but one that can be resisted, one whose course can be altered? And suppose it's precisely in history that the mystery of salvation is hidden? Suppose salvation lies in following the luminous path of truth?

But what truth?

Up to that point, all I'd heard was that truth didn't exist.

'Truth depends on your point of view,' my father told me one day. 'And given that points of view are infinite, there must be an infinite number of truths. Anyone who says he's holding the truth in one hand already has a knife in the other, ready to defend his truth. Anyone who claims to have God on his side makes the claim so he can kill you later. Remember what the Nazis had engraved on their belt buckles: *Gott mit uns*, God with us. Remember the stakes where Catholics burned alive the people who didn't think the way they did. Truth and death always walk hand in hand.'

Spurred on by my Bible reading, that weekend I finally made up my mind to leave the kibbutz and see the country.

I took a bus to Safed. When I got there, I sat down on a low wall to eat some of the provisions I'd taken from the kibbutz kitchens. Thumping music was coming from some nearby tourist bars, while a guide speaking fluent English pointed out the beauties of the place to a small group of tired, bored Americans.

'In its early centuries, Safed was above all a fortress, a stronghold of the resistance against the Roman invaders. It wasn't until the sixteenth century that Safed became one of the most important centres of Jewish mysticism. This period also saw the building of the most important synagogues, which can still be admired today.'

His words were punctuated by strange, metallic, repetitive sounds. Not far away, a child, the son of a couple no longer in their first youth, was frantically pressing the buttons of a video game. Three times, his father told him to stop. At the fourth, he snatched the game from the boy's hands, shouting angrily, in English, 'These are your roots!'

The hot air bestirred itself and rose from the plain, weakly moving the leaves of various plants. Farther off, two swans — wings spread wide, feet dangling, taking advantage of the rising air currents — flew great circles in the air.

Early in the afternoon, I took a bus down to Tiberias, on the Sea of Galilee. I expected a poor fishing village, but instead I landed in a tourist town, part Rimini and part Las Vegas. The dreariness of holiday spots in the low season had settled on the place, lingering in the smell of grease, cooked and cold; glimmering in the bright signs, with half their lights burned out; and permeating the souvenir shop where I bought a postcard.

On the back, I wrote *Here's an outpost that would suit you . . .* and sent the card to my father.

I spent that first night in a small hotel in Tiberias. The following day, I set out for the ruins of Capernaum.

The wind had come up, and threatening waves roiled the vast expanse of the lake.

I made a brief detour to visit the archaeological site of Tabgha. There were already three coaches waiting in its parking lot.

As I reached the steps leading to the site, I ran into a variegated crowd of my countrymen, for the most part retired couples whose accents suggested they were from the provinces of the Veneto. They all wore identically coloured scarves around their necks and visor caps. Many of them bore the marks of a lifetime spent working the land. Some of the women were elegantly dressed – skirt, blouse, little cardigan sweater – carrying antiquated purses and sporting permanent waves untouched by the anxieties of the new millennium.

A middle-aged cleric, probably the priest of their parish, accompanied them. He was as anxious as a school-teacher bringing her small charges on a field trip, and he kept repeating the same directions: 'Come over here . . . get closer . . . listen . . .'

But apart from the three or four parishioners who didn't budge from his side, the group seemed to pay him little attention and showed greater interest in the place's potential as a playground. The boldest of them, in fact, kicked off their shoes and waded into the lake, noisily splashing one another like a bunch of kids.

Scattered persons immortalised the scene with the most sophisticated and technologically advanced systems of visual reproduction. They focused, filmed, and photographed without ever removing their eyes from their cameras.

In the meanwhile, two other coaches had pulled up

to the shore of the lake and discharged new waves of pilgrims, this time German and Korean.

'One of the earliest historical references to this place comes from the pilgrim Egeria,' said a German guide. She had begun speaking at once, all the while holding aloft a sign with the name of her tour. 'Here's what she wrote in the year 394 AD: "Not far from Capernaum can be seen the stone steps where Our Lord stood. There also, above the level of the sea, is a grassy field where many herbs and palm trees grow. Nearby are seven springs, each flowing with abundant water . . ." Look to your left. Under that octagonal construction, you can still see the principal spring. The water – part sulphurous, part salty – flows out at thirty-two degrees Celsius. This is, therefore, a thermal spring.'

The news about the spring's salubrious qualities seemed to excite the German ladies, who quickly swarmed about searching for a rivulet they could dip a finger into, trying to recapture the same sensations they'd felt in the hot springs of Abano Terme.

The Korean group was more orderly and compact. They all turned their eyes at once to whatever their priest pointed out to them, as if they were part of a single organism.

Finally, the Italian priest's efforts were rewarded as well. After having gesticulated and raised his voice in vain, with a few blasts on a little whistle – probably the same one he used on the playing fields at the parish recreation centre – he succeeded in gathering his flock around him and read them the Gospel story set in that very place: 'In those days the multitude being very great, and having nothing to eat, Jesus called his disciples unto him, and saith unto them, "I have compassion on the multitude, because they have now been with me three days, and have nothing to eat. And if I send them away fasting to their own homes, they will faint by the way; for divers of them came from far." And his disciples say unto him, "Whence should we have so much bread in the wilderness, as to fill so great a multitude?" And Jesus saith unto them, "How many loaves have ye?" And they said, "Seven, and a few little fishes." And he commanded the multitude to sit down on the ground. And he took the seven loaves and the fishes, and gave thanks, and brake them, and gave to his disciples, and the disciples to the multitude.'

At the end of this passage, the priest raised his eyes from the page and said, 'How many of us would be capable of following Christ for days without eating? Would we be able to give proof of so much devotion just for the sake of hearing his word? And how many of us would be inclined to accept it? Does his word upset us, or is it a word we can rest upon, the way you rest on a soft pillow?'

At the end of his discourse, he exhorted his audience,

saying, 'So let's collect our thoughts for a moment of meditation and prayer that may help us understand the underlying meaning of our pilgrimage.' Some of his parishioners assumed painfully rapt expressions, while others looked around, slightly embarrassed or distracted, as if they were thinking about how long it would be before they could eat their packed lunches.

Meanwhile, the wind coming off the lake had intensified, sending a few visor caps scooting along the ancient stones; scarves flapped like flags, while from the branches of the eucalyptus trees we could hear the dry rustle of the leaves mixed with the passionate chirping of the sparrows.

I sat on the steps of the amphitheatre and attentively scrutinised the faces around me. If they chose to come all the way here, I thought, they must believe in something. Otherwise, they would have preferred to bake in the sun of the Canary Islands.

That morning, while waiting for the bus, I'd read this passage in the Gospel of St Matthew: 'The light of the body is the eye: if therefore thine eye be single, thy whole body shall be full of light.'

Was there light in those bodies, brightness in those eyes? Or rather conformism, sentimentalism, superstition? I'm doing this because it's what the others are doing, because I want to be admired for my virtue, because, no matter what, I want to be protected from the powerful forces of evil that dominate the universe, and therefore, instead of a coral horn, I wear a cross around my neck; in fact, just to be sure, I wear two of them, along with a hand of Fatima.

Was this faith, or was it exactly the form of belief that should be rejected? And what relationship was there between faith and religion? Could you practise a religion without having any faith, and vice versa? What was a heavenly gift, and what was human weakness? Where was the line between the truth and the desire for approval?

All the while I sat there, I searched for other eyes that would respond to mine, but it was like slipping on ice or Plexiglas; probably I was the lightless one, but no one in that whole crowd emitted even the tiniest reverberation.

I was on the verge of giving up when a flash met my gaze, shining from the radiant face of a tiny, elderly Korean lady. Her countrymen were already climbing back on their tour bus, but she – who knows why – came up to me with a smile and took my hand between both of hers, squeezing it hard, as if she were trying to tell me, *Keep going, don't stop*, and then, after the hint of a bow, she scurried away to the coach with small, quick steps.

Many hours later, I arrived in Capernaum. There, too, I found the usual mass of tourist buses. Guides and travel assistants, speaking various languages, filled the air with explanations, which I grasped in pieces as I moved through the brightly-coloured crowd heading in the direction of the archaeological area.

All that remained of the ancient synagogue were four white limestone columns and, on the ground, some bas-relief fragments covered with carvings of pomegranates and bunches of grapes.

'The Via Maris passed through Capernaum,' a man holding a signal paddle was saying. 'The Via Maris was the ancient road that linked Syria and Mesopotamia to Egypt and Palestine. It was a road travellers were obliged to take, especially the drivers of the long merchant cara-vans. And it was to this very synagogue that Jesus came to preach after he left Nazareth. Anyone have any idea why?'

'Because it was like a lorry parking area.'

'Or a shopping centre.'

'Exactly! Jesus must have chosen it because it was such a busy place. Later, in 665, the synagogue was destroyed, probably by an earthquake . . .'

The sun was at its zenith, and the temperature was quite hot. Following the stream of people trudging ahead in disorder, some eating sandwiches, some quenching their thirst from small bottles of mineral water, I reached a shady spot in the southernmost part of the excavations and sat down to have a snack myself.

Of the town that had been Simon Peter's birthplace, nothing was left but the foundations of the houses. I could hear the guides droning on: 'This is where St Matthew had his tax-collector's table. This is where Simon lived with his mother-in-law.'

I was wondering why, when people talk about Simon Peter, they mention only this one relative, and why his wife and children never appear, when my sight was afflicted by a kind of monstrous spaceship, a construction of glass and cement perched on six large iron feet, totally obscuring the view of the lake.

What was it?

At first glance, a low-end dance hall right out of the sixties or some bizarre temple for UFO worshippers.

'This is the site of Peter's house,' the guides kept repeating emphatically, indicating the modest remnants of a wall hidden by the dreary spaceship.

Peter's mother-in-law would have had good reason to loathe him, I thought, if she'd known he'd cause her family's memory to be crushed under tons of cement and glass. But maybe it wasn't Peter's fault, but rather the obtuse conceit of human beings, who must exhibit the signs of their power everywhere.

Dozens and dozens of coins tossed by tourists glinted on the house's ancient floor. I couldn't understand what the sense of this ritual might be. Was the gesture supposed to be propitiatory? Auspicious? Or was it perhaps the far-sighted beginning of a collection taken up to tear down that monster and return Capernaum to its enchantment some happy day not too long from now?

By then, it was late. I'd wanted to go up to the top of the Mount of Beatitudes, but I wasn't sure I'd have time to get back to the kibbutz, as I'd promised my uncle I would, so I walked back to the bus stop.

Throughout the ride, while the landscape was being gobbled up by the darkness, I reflected on the day I'd just spent. *The multitude of the wise is the salvation of the world* – I'd read that line in the Bible a short while before. Had I met any of the wise that day, or in years past?

The only priests I'd ever encountered along my way were the ones I saw on television. I don't remember anything about their sermons, except that they emanated an aura suffused with moralistic sentimentality that failed to open any door in my mind and quite possibly sealed the one to my heart.

What was Wisdom, really? Was it the shooting spinal pains I'd had forever?

So on the shores of this lake, the Sea of Galilee, the Rabbi of Nazareth fed thousands of people. Were there any loaves or fishes left to hand out? And what hunger were they supposed to satisfy? What did modern man hunger for, when he possessed everything except himself? What did the soul hunger for? For glory, triumphs, verdicts, separations? Or simply for the discovery of a threshold it could kneel before?

16

In the following months, my life took on a regular rhythm. I worked in the laundry with a group of old ladies who spoke Yiddish. While they folded the washing, I operated the sheet-ironing machine. My knowledge of German helped me to understand some of what they said and to engage in a minimum of conversation.

For the most part, I spent my free time with Uncle Jonathan; he, too, seemed happy to have recovered a missing branch of the family. In the evenings, we sat talking for hours in his little living room or went for walks along the rows of citrus trees he himself had planted.

'In the beginning,' he said, 'this work had merely been assigned to me. For a while, as far as I was concerned, planting a tree was the same as building a wall; I didn't see the difference. But as the years passed and I looked after the trees and watched them grow, I developed a real passion for them. My wife often used to tease me: "You think more about those trees than you do about your children," and maybe she was right.

'After all, a certain inevitability hovered over the children's destinies. However hard I might try to bring them up in the best possible way, I knew that at a certain point they could – in total autonomy – make a bad choice, or one simply different from mine.

'With my trees, however, things were different. They depended on my care. They required water when the soil got too dry, mineral oil to protect them from scale insects, and the right amount of fertiliser at the end of the winter, because if you got the proportions of the various composts wrong, the trees would produce too many leaves or the fruit would start falling prematurely or you could even cause dangerous burns. That's a mistake I made a lot in the beginning: I gave the soil too many nutrients. I overfed it like a nervous mother and wound up making it sick. Fertiliser has to be applied in the correct proportions and at the right time, and sometimes the right move is to apply none at all. A reasonable amount of deprivation is as good for plants as it is for children; in order to feel the desire to have something, you must first give it up.

'These days, there's a rather obtuse but widespread notion that children, if they're to be happy, must have everything right away, everything from foreign languages to computer games. I often discuss this topic with young couples, and they tell me I'm old-fashioned and maybe even a bit sadistic. They don't understand that you have to feel nostalgia for something before you can go on a journey. If I deprive my plants of light, they'll concentrate all their strength on finding it again. Their apical cells will strain spasmodically to discover a chink, and once the goal has been reached, the plant will be stronger because it's had to encounter adversity and overcome it.

'Spoiled plants, like spoiled children, have only one path ahead of them: the path of their ego.

'I make these assertions, but I know I'm alone. The modern world's evolving, but in a different way from before, and I certainly can't do anything about that. But I would like it if people would think more about trees, if they'd learn to care for them and be grateful to them, because (even though no one seems to remember this) without trees, our lives could not exist; it's their breath that allows us to breathe.

'Do you know what aspect of the modern world I'm most afraid of? The spreading sense of omnipotence. Man is convinced he can do anything because he lives in an artificial world, built with his own hands, and he believes he has total dominion over it. But whoever does what I do, whoever grows plants and trees, knows that's not the case.

'Of course, if I want to guarantee regular deliveries of water to my trees, I can construct a sophisticated irrigation system – we've cultivated practically the whole country like that – but if it doesn't rain for days, for months, for years, at some point the earth will grow so dry it'll crack, plants will die, and animals will die with them. We can't manufacture water, you see. And we can't manufacture oxygen, either. We're dependent on something that's out of our hands. If the sea rises, we'll be overwhelmed; if locusts arrive, they'll devour the harvest and the seedlings exactly the way they did in the days of the pharaohs. But those are the kinds of things we don't know any more, enclosed as we are by our artificial lights.

'The only sure horizon is that of our dominion over the material world. We're curing more and more diseases and using more and more sophisticated methods to do so. This, obviously, is an extraordinary accomplishment. But then again, we freeze pigs alive to see if it might be possible for us to fall asleep and wake up again, at several reprises, over an extended period – in short, to see whether we can counterfeit death and come back to life. We dismember the bodies of the dead and keep the pieces on ice for use as spare parts.

'See here? My kneecap hardly moves any more because of arthritis – it's always swollen, and I have a hard time walking. Do you know what a physician at the hospital said to me one day? He said, "If you want, we can replace it with another kneecap." I said, "And where are you going to get another kneecap?" And he calmly replied, "At the bank."

'In other words, somewhere in the world, there's a giant freezer that contains all possible spare parts; instead of courgettes and peas, it holds kneecaps and hands, tendons and eyes, waiting there to be used as replacements like car doors in a body shop.

'I saw the expression that came over the doctor's face when I gave him my reply, which was, "I'd rather be a cripple than profane another person's body." He looked at me in a way that let me know he thought I was just an old fanatic. But I've never been fanatical about anything. Doubt and perplexity have accompanied my every step. I would have liked to go back and tell him so, but then I realised it wasn't worth the trouble. Enclosed spaces cause incredible obtuseness in people. You have to stand out in the open in order to admit that there's something you can't understand. That new awareness isn't a defeat; it makes it possible for you to grow.

'From that point, you can go on some extraordinary journeys, as my son always says, and if you don't, whatever road you undertake to travel on will only lead you in a circle, around and around.

'When you're holding your newborn child in your

arms, how can you think he's an assembly of spare parts? You feel his tender flesh, entrusted to your care; you see his eyes – if you could read what's in them, you'd be able to understand everything – and you realise that those few pounds of matter incorporate the greatest of mysteries. It's not your intelligence that tells you this, but your guts, which have produced that mystery. Do you know this psalm? "My frame was not hidden from thee, when I was being made in secret, intricately wrought in the depths of the earth."

'And then I'm supposed to saw up those bones and put them in a freezer? No thanks, I'd rather let them go back to the depths of the earth. I'd rather think that "in thy book were written, every one of them, the days that were formed for me, when as yet there was none of them," to continue the psalm. I'd rather bow my head and accept my fate.

'I often discuss these things with my son when he and his little girls come to visit me. He and I stay up late and talk when everyone else has gone to bed. Sometimes he laughs and says I've become more religious than he is, but I tell him he's wrong, because I'm like a shop-keeper who has an account with someone, an account he hasn't settled yet – my mother's death, my father's, the extermination of millions of innocents throughout history – and since I've got that account, I can't give myself heart and soul to a faith, but by the same token,

I can't pretend there's nothing there, either. I can't say that all's well under the sun or that the heavens are filled with anything other than masses of matter in motion. Anyone who makes declarations like that either can't see or pretends not to see what's under his nose.

'Like every city boy, when I first started planting trees, I was convinced they weren't much different from posts, except they could put out leaves. As time passed and I listened to them, observed their growth, watched them get sick and die or bear fruit, I realised that they weren't much different from children, that they needed care and love but also a firm hand. I realised that every one of them, incredibly, had its own individuality – some were stronger and others were weaker, some were generous and others were stingy, and some were even capricious.

'I tended all of them with the same dedication and intensity, but they all responded differently. This made me see that they weren't posts, but creatures with a destiny unto themselves. And if there's a mystery about them, how much greater must be the mystery that envelops human beings?

'If I had reached my present age convinced I'd spent my life planting mere posts that happened to be capable of generating fruit, what would I be by this point? Foolish? Wicked? What do you think? In any case, I'd be a person who'd lived from day to day without knowing how to listen, without knowing how to look. Instead of thoughts and questions, my head would be filled with something like wet, burning leaves. The smoke from their poor combustion would have prevented me from seeing how similar the tree's destiny is to man's.'

I told Uncle Jonathan about my own passion for trees; I described the walnut tree you'd so casually had removed and the devastation that followed. It was as if a tree had been chopped down inside of me, too. The wound was always open, and my anxieties gushed forth from it continuously.

We also talked about your illness, and about how I still hadn't been able to come to terms with our relationship: too close and over-protective in my childhood, too full of conflict afterwards. The fact that you had loved me but hadn't been able to love your daughter left me hanging, suspended in utter ambivalence as far as you were concerned.

Then I told him about my father as well, and about his affair with my mother and their years in Padua. After I was finished, and perhaps by way of turning down the drama a little, we started playing the plant game.

'What kind of plant was Ilaria?' I asked Uncle Jonathan.

'Surely, some sort of aquatic plant,' he replied. 'Her floating roots didn't let her form a stalk or live a long life, but as often happens with plants of that kind, she produced a most beautiful flower.'

'How about my father?'

Taking his cues from the stories I'd told him, Uncle Jonathan compared my father to one of those plants that one sees rolling about in desert country. They don't resemble bushes so much as crowns of thorns, he said; pushed along by the wind, they dance on the sand, clamber up dunes, and roll back down, without ever stopping. Since they have neither roots nor the possibility of growing them, they can't even offer nourishment to the bees, and their destiny is an eternal and solitary drift into nothingness.

When I was a little girl, I told my uncle, I'd wanted to have the solid strength of an oak or the fragrance of a lime tree, but recently I'd changed my mind. I was as much troubled by the lime trees' imprisonment along avenues and in gardens as I was saddened by the fate of the oaks, condemned to solitude. Therefore, I now wanted to be a willow and grow my long tresses beside a river, dip my roots in the stream, listen to the sound of the current, offer the hospitality of my boughs to the nightingales and the reed warblers, and watch the kingfishers appear and disappear in the water, like little rainbows.

Then I asked him, 'How about you? What kind of tree would you like to be?'

Uncle Jonathan concentrated for a little while before answering. 'As a young man, I would have liked to be some kind of bush – a wild rose, say, or a hawthorn, or a prunus of some kind – and blend into the middle of a hedge. After I came to Israel, I would have liked to be one of those majestic cedars that grow on the slopes of Mount Hermon. But in recent years, the tree I always think about, the one I'm most nostalgic for, is one that grows back in our part of the world, the beech. I remember beeches from my excursions in the mountains: the silvery-grey trunks, covered with moss, and the leaves lighting up the air like little flames . . . So yes, there you are, now I'd like to be a beech.

'Or better yet, I feel like a beech, I am a beech, because when life's about to go out, it burns high with emotions, with memories, with feelings, just as the foliage of those trees turns to flame in the autumn.'

17

Shortly after the feast of Shavuot, someone in Italy tried to get in touch with me. The call was transferred to the dining hall, but I was already at work. When my shift was over and I finally carried an overloaded tray to a table and sat down, a young soldier handed me a note that read, 'A call from your *abba*.'

It was my father, looking for me for the second time in his life. What had prompted him to do that? I had no idea. Maybe the view of Tiberias really appealed to him, I thought, and he wants to ask me to find him a flat there, or maybe he just wants to let me know he's leaving Grado Pineta and taking up residence in some other outpost for the summer. After all, it had been more than six months since I left Italy.

Knowing him as I did, I figured it mustn't be anything urgent. I put the scrap of paper in my pocket, thinking that I'd buy a phone card and call him the next time I left the kibbutz.

That same evening, Arik, Uncle Jonathan's elder child, came for a visit from Haifa, where he worked at the university. He looked about thirty, with a bright, open face.

In my honour and in honour of the country which (except for a handful of kilometres) had given us birth, we stayed home that evening and cooked spaghetti with tomatoes. Arik described for his father the most recent exploits of his little twins, mysteriously adding that soon he'd have another piece of good news to share with him, but he wanted to wait until his wife arrived. Then he mentioned something about his sister, whom he'd met a week earlier in Beersheba; whereupon Uncle Jonathan said sadly, 'If I didn't call her, I wouldn't talk to her. She never calls me.'

'She's too caught up in her work,' Arik replied promptly. 'She never stops. She's convinced her task is to save humanity. If she keeps on like this, she's going to make herself ill.'

Uncle Jonathan shook his head. 'It's strange,' he said. 'Usually girls take after their fathers. In our case, however, she's more like her mother: practical, realistic, ready to pitch in no matter what the situation without ever getting even slightly upset.'

Arik didn't completely agree. 'That's not how it is. She pretends not to be upset so she won't have to confront the reasons why she is. She's decided that the world must go the way she wants it to go, regardless of anyone else.'

'Is she a very self-confident person?' I asked. I'd always envied people like that.

'Self-confident?' Arik repeated. 'Maybe. But she's more than confident; she's authoritarian. Once she's made up her mind about something, the discussion is over; whatever she's decided must necessarily be right. It's really a form of fragility.'

I asked Arik many questions about his life in Arad, and he described it to me in some detail. In the beginning, he said, it hadn't been easy for him to settle in – the climate and the landscape were completely different from what he'd known – but now he couldn't live anywhere else. He needed the stones and the clean, dry air and the flowers that grew in the wadis, the ones that exploded into a symphony of colours after the first rain. He always took his daughters to see those flowers, even though the girls were still little and couldn't really understand. He wanted to accustom them, from the start, to delighting in natural wonders.

'In the tropics, you probably get tired of flowers and end up not noticing them, but a desert that bursts into bloom only once is an unexpected gift. It makes us realise how much light is shut up inside matter.'

Then he told me the story of the siege of the fortress at Masada and mentioned that the week before, he'd seen two Japanese tourists on a bicycle pedal all the way up to the top of the fortress. He also talked about the oasis of Ein Gedi, near Masada, where even some leopards lived (if you walked up the wadi at dawn, sometimes it was possible to see them), and about the cave where David hid from Saul. If I'd like to go to Arad one day, he said, he'd take me to visit all those places.

Around eleven o'clock, Uncle Jonathan went to bed, and Arik and I went out for a walk.

After a couple of turns around the cowsheds, we started walking along the edge of the citrus orchards. The orange blossoms had opened, and they were diffusing an extraordinarily intense perfume into the mild night air. We sat down on a rock, the same one I had selected for my meditations, and talked all night long about many things: about our families, about his grandfather and his tragic end, about how he, Arik, had been troubled ever since childhood by the fact that Ottavio had loved beauty without loving Him who established it in our hearts.

'Beauty and harmony,' Arik said, 'exist to the extent that we're able to perceive them and delight in them. That's the only way for them to become nourishment for the soul. Otherwise, they're only a dazzling distraction, like the flashing hazard lights of a stopped car we have to drive around; they inevitably cause us to deviate from our intentions, to blend white and black, to transform everything into a grey sludge.

'The heart is where the battle takes place. There, good intentions and bad intentions engage each other in a no-holds-barred contest. We have to be aware of this; otherwise, we'll wind up surrendering without even putting up a fight, succumbing to the opacity of the indistinct, which is the great enemy of our time. Opacity takes the joy out of life, deprives the things around us of light, and consigns our existence to darkness.'

Around us, jackals howled to one another, occasionally accompanied for a few bars by a barking dog. Then the roosters started to crow, saluting the arrival of the new day.

Arik pointed to a little tree tied to a stake. 'Like trees,' he said, 'we have a natural desire to rise up, to ascend. Maybe it's buried under a large pile of debris, but it exists. It's a kind of nostalgia that dwells in the deepest part of every human being. Life, however, is messy and filled with conflict, and if we confide uniquely in our own judgement, we risk going in the wrong direction and being dazzled by some fake sun. That's why the Torah exists; like that young tree's stake, it helps us to rise up straight, to grow toward heaven without being broken by windstorms.'

From amid the branches of the trees came the rustling sound of sparrows' wings. As the birds woke up, their chirping grew louder and louder.

The darkness in the east steadily gave way to the light. The bright azure was already changing into orange-gold when Arik stood up and, in a low voice, started praying. I imitated him and stood beside him, but I didn't know what to say. No one had ever taught me a prayer. I searched desperately for some word that would give voice to my state of mind.

The hoopoes had already begun their erratic flight through the rows of trees when a prayer of thanks finally rose to my lips. Thanks for life, thanks for splendour, thanks for the ability to apprehend it.

The following week, I received another telephone call from Italy, but this one wasn't from my father.

It was the Mestre police, calling to announce their discovery of a dead man in an underground passage near Marghera. His name was Massimo Ancona, and in his jacket pocket they'd found a letter addressed to his daughter, with my telephone number. Did I know him? Was I really his daughter? His documents contained no mention of her, but if the implied relationship was in fact true, I was enjoined to present myself at the Mestre morgue as soon as possible to identify the body.

That same afternoon, I went to Haifa to make an airline reservation. The first available seat was on a Tel Aviv–Milan flight three days later. I booked a ticket and returned to the kibbutz.

That night, I couldn't sleep a wink. I cursed myself for not having called him back. The police couldn't or wouldn't tell me how he died, so I suspected he might have killed himself: in desperation, maybe, having tried in vain to tell me something, and I hadn't returned his call. Even though he'd never felt any sense of responsibility for my beginning, I nonetheless felt responsible for his end.

It took the wisdom of morning to make me realise how absurd such thoughts were. My father, protected as he'd always been by his unaffectionate nature and his selfishness, would never have killed himself because of an unreturned telephone call.

The following day, I was too upset to perform my usual tasks, so I took a bus to the Mount of Beatitudes.

It was lunchtime when I arrived. The big gardens surrounding the basilica were almost deserted. Below in the distance, the Sea of Galilee gleamed like a bright, bright mirror, while the wind occasionally carried up the sounds of the approaching cars on the road below.

Within those few dozen kilometres, Jesus had spent

a significant part of his brief existence. The crowd was following him everywhere; every step of the way, there were people begging him to heal them. It wasn't hard for me to imagine how exhausted and solitary he must have felt, constantly importuned by petitioners. After thirty years of silence, he spent three years immersed in constant confusion.

Besides, what did that mean, 'heal them'? To make them see, or walk, or feel differently, but to what end? To have a good appetite, to sleep better, to be able to run fast? Or maybe to reach a new level of awareness? And what connection was there between the cloying words I'd heard from the TV priests and the force, the rigour, the severity of those pronounced by the rabbi of Nazareth? One day, would those words be able to heal me, too?

I walked along the pathways, following the white marble tablets incised with the Beatitudes. Everything was in luxuriant blossom around me, and the golden orioles hurled their songs into the air as though they were questions. When I read *Blessed are the merciful, for they shall obtain mercy*, I thought about my father. Where was he now? Was he hovering nearby, watching me, or had he sunk into some dark place from which he would never emerge? Would there be mercy for the sterility of his life? What was an act of mercy, really? Wasn't it a participation in the compassion of Him who created us?

Arik's words came back to me: 'The strictness of the law and divine mercy always walk side by side, but in the most important decisions, mercy always gets the upper hand; it's impossible for a mother to be pitiless towards the child born out of her womb.'

The notion of God's maternity had struck me profoundly.

'But in the end, what does He want from us?'

'He wants growth, transformation, repentance. He wants to live in our hearts, as we, from the beginning, live in His. It's not power He desires to share with us, but fragility.'

18

Two days later, Uncle Jonathan drove me to Ben Gurion Airport in a clapped-out Subaru.

We said goodbye with a long embrace. I invited him to visit me in Trieste, and he promised to come as soon as possible; naturally, my invitation included Arik and his family.

The flight was uneventful.

In Milan, I took the train for Venice and got off at Mestre. Immediately after I presented myself at police headquarters, a young corporal accompanied me to the morgue. As we walked, he explained that an autopsy had already been performed, and that my father had died of natural causes. From one moment to the next, his heart had stopped beating.

At the morgue, the person in charge went ahead to

show us the way. Her rubber clogs produced a strange sucking sound on the linoleum floor.

A draft of frigid air struck me as I entered the cold chamber. Three corpses were lying on stainless-steel tables. He was on the middle one. His feet were sticking out from under the green sheet – it was the first time I'd even seen him without shoes – and one arm was hanging down.

The morgue official lifted the sheet. 'Do you recognise him?'

Instead of his usual sneering smile, his lips were parted in what looked like an expression of astonishment.

'Yes,' I said. 'He's my father, Massimo Ancona.'

'I'm sorry,' the corporal said.

'So am I,' I replied, and that was the moment when I felt the tears running down my cheeks.

While the young policeman filled out some forms, the morgue official, impatient to leave the cold room, chewed her gum vigorously. Her working mandibles produced the only sound in the unreal silence.

On an impulse, I grabbed the white hand hanging down from under the sheet and squeezed it. The skin felt cold like a snake's, the weight and density not much different from those of a living hand, and the fingernails had been trimmed hastily.

'Here's your last outpost,' I whispered, bending down

to kiss him, and then I added, 'Thanks, nevertheless. Thanks for the life you gave me.'

I took the train to Trieste. After I got home, I opened the plastic bag the police had turned over to me. Inside I found the keys to his house and car, a regional motorway pass (which had expired a month previously), a small address book, a wallet with worn edges, and a white envelope with my name written on it.

The wallet contained a few coins, a 50,000-lire note, two 5,000-lire notes, a national health insurance card, a little card from a supermarket in Monfalcone with stamps (he had only four to go) accumulated towards the longed-for prize: a towelling bathrobe, and, sticking out from a side compartment, a little photograph, showing its age. An elegant woman, not tall, distractedly holding a child's hand, stared at the photographer with an expression between haughty and annoyed. The picture must have been taken in Venice, in the Piazza San Marco or on the banks of the Grand Canal, facing the Giudecca. The child, a little boy, was smiling and pointing at something that had surprised him. A ship? Some seabird he'd never seen? The mother's ego, her unique focus on herself, shone through her eyes, while the boy's pupils gleamed with insatiable, joyous curiosity. On the back of the photo, written in ink faded by time, these words: *Venice*

1936. Mama and I on the embankment. Massimo Ancona and his mother, the philosophy of language professor and the indefatigable canasta player, my father and my grandmother, closed up in a wallet like the great majority of common mortals.

The name of a restaurant in Monselice was imprinted on the green plastic cover of the address book, which contained only a few telephone numbers. Under D, the doctor's and the dentist's numbers; under T, the numbers of three or four trattorias; here and there, contact information for some publishing houses and two or three feminine names; and on the first page, my number in Trieste, and below it, written in pencil in a more tremulous hand, my number in Israel.

The same unsteady hand had scrawled my name on the front of the envelope. I opened it. Inside were two yellowing sheets of paper (with the letterhead of a hotel in Cracow), filled with writing on both sides.

Grado Pineta, 13 May

I don't know whether this letter will ever come into your hands — if you're reading it, that means I'm no longer a part of this world. You know how much I detest sentimentality; nevertheless, I can't help writing you these lines. After all, you were the unhoped-for.

The dreaded and the unhoped-for.

You arrived at the end of my days, and, like one of those plants that thrust out their thin (and extremely forceful) roots to colonise the surrounding territory, you opened a crack in my life with your eyes, your voice, your questions, and ever since then, those eyes, that voice, those questions — I've been unable to free myself from them.

Is it the call of the blood or the weakness of senility? I don't know. I don't have enough strength or time left to answer you. It's not very important, all in all. At this point, I don't have to defend myself or explain anything any more.

Today I tried to kill myself.

There's nothing remarkable or melodramatic about this. The decision eventually to take my own life is one I made when I first began to use my reason. Since we haven't chosen to be born, determining where and how we die is the only true freedom granted us. My body is in obvious decline, and unfortunately my mind is following right behind it.

This morning, the security shutter on the window to my room broke, and I couldn't open it. I stayed in the dark until five o'clock in the afternoon, uselessly trying to track down the repairman by telephone. His office kept saying things like, 'Try calling back a little later, or we'll call you,' but nothing happened, so in the end I decided to take a walk. I stepped out into the soft May air, accompanied by the tireless flights of birds bringing food to their nests; I saw little yellow flowers everywhere, growing up out of cracks in the cement. The month of May, I thought, is the most extraordinary time of year to leave the earth forever, the time that requires the most nerve, because that's when life is in the fullness of its splendour. It can't take much courage to kill yourself in November, when the sky is covered with gloomy rain clouds. Now, you may think depression has pushed me to this point, but in fact I'm completely lucid and fully aware of my choice.

After I got home, I tried to call you. I wanted to hear your voice one last time, but I had no luck. At the other end of the line, there was a succession of different people, speaking a little English, a little Hebrew, and a little Spanish, but none of them managed to find you.

Then I climbed up on a chair to retrieve my revolver, which has been on top of the bookshelf, wrapped in a dark cloth, for many years. I loaded the gun and waited for the night to end, reading my favourite poems. I had no wish to die inside, like a rat; I wanted to take my leave in an open space, facing the sea, to watch the dawn one more time, to see the sun coming up and flooding the world with light.

Around four o'clock, I went down to the beach. As I walked along in the darkness, I could hear the seashells crunching under my shoes. I sat down on the same rowboat you chose one day when we stopped to rest. I could feel the cold metal against my thighs.

A little after five, the eastern sky over Trieste and Istria began to lighten. The air was filled with the cries of seabirds, and the sea, still at low tide, lapped gently at the shore. I looked around and slipped the revolver out of my pocket, waiting. When the top of the orange disc showed over the horizon, I pointed the gun at my temple and pulled the trigger. There was a loud click, and nothing happened. I rotated the cylinder and tried again: another click.

In the meantime, a pensioner and his two poodles had appeared on the beach. He threw a coloured ball into the air, and the dogs chased after it, barking happily. I can't even kill myself, I thought, putting the revolver back in my pocket.

A few hours later, the shutter repairman arrived and brought light into my room. That afternoon, I went to Monfalcone to do a bit of shopping. Life goes on, I don't know for how much longer, but it goes on, I thought as I dropped the revolver into a drawer. I'll wait until fate runs its course.

In the evening, I stood on the little kitchen balcony. The temperature was almost summery, warm enough to ferment the algae in the lagoon and saturate the air with briny vapours. The lights were on in a flat in the building across from mine; a woman with an apron and a bucket was giving the place a thorough clean, getting ready for the imminent tourist season.

I was going back inside when a sudden brightness caught my eye among the unkempt shrubs that divide the two buildings. Fireflies. It had been years since I'd seen fireflies. They were dancing between the ground and the bushes, stitching the air with their intermittent glow. Just the previous day, I would have smiled at the cunning of nature's reproductive strategies; what else could that light be but an extraordinary stratagem for engaging in copulation?

But that evening, all at once, everything seemed different. I no longer felt irritated at the housewife who was cleaning her floors; I no longer saw the fireflies' little ignis fatuus *as part of a mechanical process.*

There's no cunning in that light, but rather wisdom, I said to myself, and I began to cry. Nearly sixty years had passed since the last time I'd done that, on the ship that was taking us to Brazil.

I wept slowly, in silence, without sobs; I wept for those little sparks, enveloped in the tyranny of night, and for their unsteady motion, because suddenly it was clear to me that in every darkness there lives, compressed, a fragment of light.

Am I making you laugh? Do I seem pathetic? Maybe so. These words will probably aggravate the unextinguished rage of your youth, but I've reached the point where nothing matters any more. And so I'll cover myself with even more ridicule by telling you that throughout these past months, I've lived with the hope of seeing you again.

You know I've always followed a policy of honesty (even though it has sometimes done me harm). In these present days, in the remaining time that fate has granted me, I've freed myself from my pride, and I have the possibility of reflecting on things without fear, because basically, I'm already dead; I can feel the sheet on my body and the moist earth covering me. Precisely because I'm in the beyond (and no longer afraid of ridicule), I can tell you that it was fear that determined my days; what I called boldness was actually nothing but panic. I was afraid that things wouldn't go the way I'd decided they should. I was afraid of passing some limit — not a mental limit, but a limit of the heart. I was afraid of loving and of not being loved in return.

In the end, that's man's only real terror, and it's the reason why he gives himself over to pettiness.

Love, like a bridge suspended over the void . . .

Out of fear, we complicate simple things. In order to follow the phantoms of our minds, we transform a straight path into a labyrinth we don't know how to escape.

It's so difficult to accept the rigours of simplicity, the humility of trusting.

What else have I done my whole life long besides this: run away from myself, run away from responsibilities, wound others before they could wound me?

When you read these lines (and I'm in a refrigerated room or the cold ground), know that in my last days I was inhabited by a feeling of sadness — a melancholy sadness, without anger, and perhaps for that reason even more painful.

Pride, humility; in the end, those are the only two things being weighed in the balance. I don't know what their specific weights are, so I can't say whether or not a day of humility can suffice to redeem a life of pride.

It would have been wonderful to be able to give you a hug, little time bomb, who turned up by surprise (and too late) to ravage my life. Even if this doesn't make up for anything, I wanted to hold

you one last time, long and hard, and inside that
embrace there would have been all the hugs I never
gave you, the ones from when you were born and
when you were little and when you were growing up,
and the ones you'll need when I'm not around any
more.

Forgive the obtuseness of the sneering man who
brought you into the world.

Papa

The funeral took place a week later, in the Jewish cemetery in Trieste. Aside from the members of the minyan
and the rabbi, I was the only one there. The recital of
the Kaddish was barely over when the noon siren went
off, very loudly, in the nearby shipyards.

There weren't many people in the graveyard on that
hot summer day. Instead of going home, I walked up to
the Catholic cemetery. I stopped at the stalls by the
entrance before I went in and bought a bunch of pretty
sunflowers.

During the winter, the bora had carried many leaves,
together with various advertising flyers, into our little
family mortuary chapel, now long neglected. The air
inside was suffocating, and there was an odour of damp
and mildew; it had been years since anyone had done
any cleaning in there. I opened the door wide and set
off to buy a broom and a cloth. When the job was done,

I put the flowers in the vase and sat down to keep you company for a while.

Who can tell where you were and how you were? Maybe, at least on the other side, you and my mother had met; maybe you two had finally managed to dispel the shadows that kept you from having a serene relationship. Maybe you and she could see me from up there, sitting on your tomb on a summer afternoon. Maybe it's true that the dead have the power to stand beside the living and protect them without ever letting them out of their sight. Or is that just a wish of ours, one of our all-too-human hopes? Is it true that on the other side there really is a judgement, with the light-fingered archangel Michael holding up the delicate scales? And how are the units of measurement established? Is the specific weight the same for every act? Are there only two categories – good and evil – or are the listings a bit more complex? How much do the sufferings of an innocent weigh? Is the violent death of a just man worth the same as the passing of an evil man who dies full of days? Why do the wicked often enjoy long, untroubled lives – as if someone were protecting them – while the gentle must endure insults and adversity? The longevity granted to unscrupulous men – could that be a sign of divine mercy, which allows them to live so long in order to have more time to repent and convert their hearts?

And sorrow, what's the weight of sorrow?

My mother's sorrow, my father's, yours, Uncle Ottavio's, and mine (when I die) – what happens to all that sorrow? Does it turn to inert dust, or nourishment? Wouldn't it be better if one could lead a carefree life, no questions asked? What becomes of the man who never interrogates himself, who has no doubts?

Arik spoke to me about the inclination to good and evil that's in every one of us, of the struggle that's constantly taking place in our heart. To live a life of inertia, no questions asked – isn't that tantamount to giving yourself over to the banal mechanics of existence, to the inexorable law of gravity, always and forever dragging us down? Don't doubts and questions arise from nostalgia? As the apical cells always and forever drive plants upward, searching for light, so must questions drive us humans towards heaven. Sorrow, confusion, the devastation of evil – couldn't they be, perhaps, the consequences of our veering off course?

One of the people I met in Israel was Miriam, a French survivor of Auschwitz, who oversaw the kibbutz's little library. On one arm, she wore several jangling bracelets, and on the other, the violet tattoo of her number. I couldn't take my eyes off it.

'Does it upset you?' she asked me.

'Yes,' I replied, frankly and honestly.

On the basis of that reciprocal openness, we formed a friendship. At the outbreak of the war, she said, she was a twenty-two-year-old biology student, one year away from her degree. 'My father was a man with very advanced ideas for those times. He was rather old when I was born, but healthy. He was a doctor, and he always encouraged my curiosity. To his great joy, I was fascinated by living things right from the start, beginning when I was a little girl. I loved to observe, question, experiment. While my schoolmates were losing themselves in boring fairytales, I was off on a solitary voyage among mitochondria and enzymes; their processes were the only magic that took my breath away. My idol was Madame Curie; I knew every passage of her biography by heart. I wanted to become someone like her and put my intellect at the service of humanity. I always had a passion for analysing and discussing things. As a student – inflamed by the atmosphere that prevailed in those days – I loved to expose the senselessness and folly of the world.

'History, however, gave me a brutal push in a completely different direction. I saw my mother and my father on their way to death; we gazed into one another's eyes for the last time before they disappeared into the building where the "showers" were. A few months later, I was supposed to die, too, in the reprisals for an escape attempt, but someone stepped forward and took my place, a man who opposed his serenity to my girlish terror.

'I'm here because he went up in smoke. What else

could I be but a witness, someone who has never stopped thinking about that step? All the questions are contained in those modest thirty centimetres: one step taken, another held back.'

We'd sit in the coolest corner of the library and talk for hours about death, about how the heart of Europe was turned to ashes in only six years.

'Everyone says, where was God? Why didn't he put an end to the slaughter with a flick of his finger? Why didn't he send a rain of fire and brimstone down upon the evildoers?' Miriam often repeated those questions, and her answer was, 'But I say, Where was man? Where was the creature fashioned "a little below the angels"? Because men built the gas chambers; in order to optimise the time factor, specialist engineers calculated the exact angle at which the rail carts delivering bodies to the ovens should turn; nothing could interrupt the rhythms of disposal. They made their calculations while the wife was knitting in the living room and the kids were in their flannel pyjamas, asleep in their little beds, clutching teddy bears. It was men who went from house to house, rousting people out, dislodging them from the most hidden places. It was men who drenched their hands in blood, kicked newborn babies to death, slaughtered old people. Men who had the power to choose and had not chosen. Men who, instead of seeing other men as people, saw them only as objects.'

Another time, as she was dusting the library's tiny book collection with the kind of tenderness one shows towards children, Miriam said, 'You know what the biggest trap is? Everyone's convinced the Holocaust is a phenomenon circumscribed by time. People are continually having ceremonies where they repeat in chorus, with proper firmness, "Never again! Never again will such a horror descend on the earth!" But when the buboes of the plague appear, what happens? Does the sick person get well and the epidemic abruptly stop? Or does it spread, becoming more and more virulent, producing the bacteria that will eventually carry the contagion everywhere?

'Instead of "Never again", we must have the courage to say, "Still and always!" Because still and always, under the appearance of normality, the miasma of those years pollutes our days, preparing us for a holocaust of cosmic dimensions. And society is the place to exercise technical perfection.

'In Auschwitz, nothing was left to chance, there was no wastage and no lost time. The pure mechanism was all that existed. The central organisation took care of everything. At the end of this meticulous programming, the perfect man would finally be born, the only one capable of dominating the world and the only one worthy of living in it.

'Things don't change that much. Aren't there people

now, trying to convince us that our society can become as perfect as ant society? Are bees and ants really the models we ought to use? Do we have antennae or little feelers or prismatic eyes?

'The flames of communism's funeral pyre aren't completely extinguished yet, nor are its wounds completely healed, when already we're hearing about the prospect of a new paradise on earth: a world without disease or death, without deformities or imperfections.

'The paradise of the apprentice wizards. "We've got everything under control," they shout on the world's televisions and in the world's newspapers, when anybody who stops and thinks, if only for a moment, knows that we control nothing. Neither the possibility of being born nor the moment of death (unless you inflict it on yourself). Neither the water that comes down from the sky nor the quakes that split the earth.

'These complexities escape the apprentice wizards, shut up inside their sanitised chambers as they are, and convinced that the universe consists of the microns of reality that dominate their thoughts. That's why they can so merrily mix up the genetic patrimonies of different species in the name of progress (which is visible only to them and to the multinational companies that sign their patents) and why they can clone flowers and animals. And surely, in the obscure secrecy of some laboratory, they're already cloning humans. After all, it would be so convenient to have a copy of yourself at your disposal – in case of breakdowns, you could use it for spare parts.

'The wizards' weapon is altruistic persuasion. They manipulate people's good faith by convincing them that all this devastation is carried out exclusively for humanitarian motives. How will the world's billions of poor eat without the new seeds invented by man for man? But I say what about the seeds invented by God? Aren't they enough? Hasn't an extraordinary complexity already been put at our service? And isn't it, just maybe, our inability to see this complexity that drives us to seek new horizons that are actually horizons of death?

'When man dreams about making a world without pain, without imperfections, in reality he's already rolling out the barbed wire and dividing the world into the suitable and the unsuitable, a world in which the members of that second group are hardly different from ballast, something that will need to be cast off along the way.

'Naturally, I believe what Madame Curie believed – man's mission *is* to care for his neighbour in need – but when the care turns into a delirium of omnipotence, when it gets tangled up with the struggle for billion-dollar patents, then it turns into something very different from the proper aspirations of the human race. Instead of applauding the grand promises of science, we should have the courage to ask questions, even if they make us as unpopular as Jeremiah: Without disease, without fragility, without uncertainty, what does man turn into? And what becomes of his neighbour? Are we perfectible machines or troubled creatures in exile? Can our ultimate meaning be found in omnipotence, or in the acceptance of our precariousness? Out of precariousness, questions arise; a sense of mystery and wonder can grow from questions, but what can omnipotence and certainty generate?

'Aren't they trying to turn the human race into a multitude of omnivorous, perennially unsatisfied consumers? I buy, therefore I am. This is the horizon we're all moving towards, as docile as lambs, except that our goal isn't the sheepfold; it's the abyss. And idolatry lies sleeping, always ready to awaken, in the heart of man.

'Unimaginable catastrophes are waiting for us just around the corner. How is it possible to think we can touch the core of the atom, manipulate DNA, and still keep going forward? While everyone's dancing with their headphones on and their eyes closed in artificial ecstasy, I see the flashes of the coming end, getting closer and closer every day.'

We watched a hoopoe walk past the window, shaking its crest.

'Can't anything be done?' I asked.

Miriam turned toward me and stared at me for a long time in silence – what depths did the light of her eyes come from? – and then she said, 'Of course. We must repent and open our hearts and minds to His word. Chase away the gods who've been carousing in our hearts for too long. Instead of the law of ego, we'd have to observe the law of the covenant.'

'But isn't the law a cage?'

'Oh no,' she said with a smile. 'The law's the only place where love can grow . . .'

A meow interrupted my memories. An extremely thin cat was at the chapel door, looking in. Her tail was as skinny as a pencil. I called her and she came in. She even let me scratch her under her chin, purring all the while with a look of ecstasy on her face.

Outside the sun had passed its highest point, and the air in the chapel was stifling hot. Before leaving, I gently touched the stone where your name's engraved. Then I passed on to Mamma's, with her two dates recording the brief span of her years.

For a while, the cat followed me as I walked to the cemetery entrance, but then she disappeared behind a stone. The only flowers that stood with dignity in their vases were made of plastic; all the others drooped heavily, exhausted by the great heat. Dozens of wasps were buzzing around a tap, colliding furiously with one another while hopefully waiting for a drop of water.

Before I left the cemetery, I turned around to

contemplate its grounds (which also contained the Jewish and Turkish cemeteries) one last time. All of you – you, my mother, my father – were there while the unknown spaces of life were opening up before me; for better or worse, all of you taught me a great deal; and somehow, your mistakes had provided me with a treasure.

I went back home and returned to my cleaning.

I opened all the windows to let out the closed-in smell; the summer light streamed in forcefully, illuminating the darkest corners. I went into your room to get some clean sheets. The linen cupboard was in perfect order; for some reason, it had escaped the fury of your disease. The little sachets of lavender I saw you make up, most skilfully, so many times were still scattered here and there. When I reached for some sheets, the ones with the embroidered monogram, I saw a big yellow envelope lying on top of them. You'd written on it, in an unsteady hand, *For you.*

I'd never seen it before. How long had it been there? Since before you got really ill? Or maybe from before then, from the period of half-gestures, when for reasons unknown even to you your actions suddenly struck out down a different path? I opened the envelope and saw that it contained a large notebook with a flowery cover. At that moment, however, I didn't feel ready to face whatever might be inside, and so I laid the notebook on the kitchen table and kept cleaning until well past noon.

That day, while working furiously, I came to two important decisions. The first concerned a dog: I would go to the pound the next day and pick out another one, because I couldn't bear looking at that empty garden. The second decision concerned my future; in the autumn, I would enrol in the university and study forest science, because I'd finally realised what it was I wanted to do for the rest of my life: take care of trees.

After the hottest part of the day had passed, I started watering the garden. The rose bush was at the end of its flowering and seemed not to have suffered too much from my absence, while the hydrangeas looked pretty badly off. I watered them for a long time, now and then aiming the hose high so that I could watch the stream of water turn into a shower of golden droplets.

When I was done, I took out a deckchair, put it in the middle of the garden, and sat down with an orangeade in one hand and your notebook in the other.

Opicina, 16 November, 1992 was written at the top of the first page.

I recognised your handwriting, as tidy and regular as always.

You have been away for two months, and for two months I have heard nothing from you apart from a postcard telling me that you were still alive . . .